“Something happ[illegible] ing changed betwee[illegible]

No, Delia wanted [illegible]
they both knew it.

“We can’t let that happen.” She needed to maintain the balance of power. Rebuild some guise of professionalism before it was too late. “This job is too important to me.”

“And your professional skills are valuable to me, as well. But we can work around that. Besides, do you really believe ignoring it will make it go away, Delia?”

“If we both make an effort, yes. Of course. We’re both adults with professional agendas. We can keep those work goals front and center when we’re together.”

“Like we did today.”

“Today was an aberration.” It had to be. “Emotions ran high. We were both scared for Emily.” She wanted it to be as simple as that. “Just an adrenaline moment.”

“So what about this moment, right now?” he asked. “Adrenaline?”

She willed a logical answer to explain the way the air simmered all around them.

Any answer she might have given was a moot point, however, since Jager chose that moment to lower his lips to hers.

* * *

Little Secrets: His Pregnant Secretary is part of the Little Secrets series:

Untamed passion, unexpected pregnancy...

Dear Reader,

I am having so much fun following the lives of the McNeills! I was as shocked as anyone when Dad announced his "other" family, and knew I needed to hunt down all the brothers. This family—abandoned young by their part-time father—has been through a lot and they are fiercely protective of one another.

That's a protectiveness Jager McNeill extends to his assistant, Delia, after an unexpected night of passion. He won't abandon his child the way his father abandoned him. For Delia, her boss's insistence on keeping her close wreaks havoc on her desire for independence. But resisting the passion of a McNeill isn't easy. Especially when she finds herself falling in love...

Don't forget to visit joannerock.com for updates on The McNeill Magnates and sneak peeks at what's up next!

Happy Reading!

Joanne Rock

JOANNE ROCK

LITTLE SECRETS: HIS PREGNANT SECRETARY

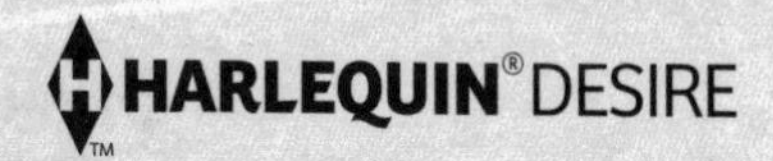

ISBN-13: 978-0-373-83887-5

Little Secrets: His Pregnant Secretary

This edition published by arrangement with Harlequin Books S.A.

For questions and comments about the quality of this book, please contact us at CustomerService@Harlequin.com.

Printed in U.S.A.

Four-time RITA® Award nominee **Joanne Rock** has penned over seventy stories for Harlequin. An optimist by nature and a perpetual seeker of silver linings, Joanne finds romance fits her life outlook perfectly—love is worth fighting for. A former Golden Heart® Award recipient, she has won numerous awards for her stories. Learn more about Joanne's imaginative Muse by visiting her website, joannerock.com, or following @joannerock6 on Twitter.

Books by Joanne Rock

Harlequin Desire

Little Secrets: His Pregnant Secretary

Bayou Billionaires

His Secretary's Surprise Fiancé
Secret Baby Scandal

The McNeill Magnates

The Magnate's Mail-Order Bride
The Magnate's Marriage Merger
His Accidental Heir

Visit her Author Profile page at Harlequin.com, or joannerock.com, for more titles.

For my sister-in-law, Kate,
thank you for joining our family!
My brother is lucky to have you, and so are we.
Wishing you much love and happiness.

One

Sun glinted off the brilliant blue Atlantic, full of sailboats bobbing on the calm water. For Delia Rickard, the picturesque island scene meant only one thing. It was the perfect day to ask for a raise.

Delia mentally gave herself a pep talk as she rushed around the marina in Le François, Martinique. She anticipated meeting her boss at any moment. Her father desperately needed her help and that meant forcing herself to push for that raise. Her quiet nature and organizational skills made her great at her job but sometimes posed a challenge when it came time to stand up for herself.

She hadn't seen Jager McNeill in the last six months. Would he be impressed with the changes she'd made both at his family's marina and the nearby McNeill mansion where she'd taken over as on-site property manager a year ago, on top of her responsibilities assisting Jager?

She'd worked tirelessly for months just to be worthy of Jager McNeill's trust in her. He'd given her the job as a favor since she didn't have a four-year degree—showing more faith in her than anyone else in her life. At first, it had been enough to work hard to repay Jager for giving her a chance. But now, considering the hours she put in to manage both properties and the effort she made to execute every facet to the best of her ability, she knew it was time to approach her employer about a bump up in her paycheck. Her father couldn't afford his portion of the taxes on the Rickard family lands this year and Delia needed to help to keep the small plot in the family. Her former fiancé had tried to trick her out of her share of the land once and she wouldn't give his greedy corporate backers any chance to swoop in now and take it from her or her dad. But unless she made more money, the Rickard home would be up for auction by springtime.

Delia sidestepped a family loading their cooler onto a skippered sailboat as she hurried toward the dockmaster's office for an update. Just as she got there, guests on one of the new superyachts dialed up its sound system far more than the noise regulations allowed, alerting Delia to a sunset party just getting underway.

"Cyril?" she called into the small office, raising her voice to be heard. "Any word on Mr. McNeill's arrival?"

The sun-weathered dockmaster turned to her. "His seaplane just landed. The skiff picked him up a moment ago."

"Thank you." She smiled quickly before turning to glare out toward the party boat, wishing the group would take their ten-decibel fun out to sea for a few hours. She wanted Jager's arrival to be perfect. "I'll go speak to our guest about the noise."

Cyril shouldered his way out of his office. He shaded his eyes to peer down the dock past the multimillion-dollar boat blasting house music, toward the open water. "Do you know why Jager wants to meet here?"

Delia had been puzzled about that too. Why would their boss want to step off a plane and go straight to work after being away from home for over six months?

The McNeill family had been through a harrowing year. The three brothers, Jager, Damon and Gabriel, had all relocated to Los Altos Hills, California, a year ago to establish their tech company in the heart of Silicon Valley. The software start-up had been Damon's brainchild, but both Jager and Gabriel played roles in managing the business as it grew. Shortly afterward, Damon had married. He planned to stay out West once the company took root, and Gabe and Jager would return to Martinique, where the family had a small hotel resort and the marina, in addition to the main house they sometimes rented out for upscale corporate retreats.

But then their lives had been turned upside down when Damon's new bride was kidnapped and held for ransom. All of Damon's focus had turned to getting his wife back, leaving Jager and Gabe to run the fledgling business. Eight months after the kidnapping—even after ransom had been paid—Caroline McNeill had not been returned. Damon's father-in-law insisted the ransom note had been a hoax and that Caroline had left of her own volition. Damon refused to accept that story even though police refused to investigate. Damon had left the country and hadn't been heard from since. To save his brother's company before the value dropped with rumors of instability in the leadership, Jager had quietly shopped the software start-up to potential buyers. He hoped to sell the business as soon as possible.

"I'm not sure why he wants to visit the marina first," Delia answered Cyril, her gaze trained on the water for signs of Jager's arrival. "Maybe after the year his family has had, work is the only thing getting them through the days."

Someone had threatened her family once and Delia had never forgotten the bite of betrayal. She couldn't imagine the pain the McNeills had been through.

"I just hope he doesn't decide to sell the marina too," Cyril admitted before he retreated into the dockside office, leaving Delia with a new worry to add to her list.

It was bad enough she needed to ask for a raise. What would she do if Jager unloaded his Martinique assets?

Delia felt the thrum of bass in the repetitive techno-crap blaring from the deck speakers as she rushed up the long wooden dock as fast as her wedge-heeled sandals would allow. The superyacht had only been docked at Le François for three days and Cyril had already talked to them once about the noise and the parties.

"Excuse me!" Delia called up to the bow, which was at least ten feet above her head. She waved her arms to try to catch someone's attention. A handful of swimsuit-clad couples lounged on big built-in sofas or milled around the bar. A few kids ran around the deck, squealing and chasing each other. "Hello!"

Delia backed up a step to make herself visible to the group. She could hardly hear herself shout; they were completely oblivious. She glanced behind her to make sure she had more clearance, well aware that the docks were narrow at the far end where the larger watercraft tied off.

She peered back up at the party boat just in time to see one of the kids—a girl in a fluttery white bathing suit cover-up—lose her balance near the rail. Her scream pierced the air right before she pitched headlong into the water with a splash.

Terrified and not sure if anyone else even saw the

child go in, Delia scrambled to the edge of the dock. She toed off her shoes and tugged her phone out of the pocket of her simple sundress, never taking her eyes off the ring of rippling water where the girl had landed. Jumping in feetfirst to avoid hitting her head on any hidden debris, Delia rotated her arms to pull herself deeper.

Salt water stung her eyes when she tried to open them. Her hair tangled in her face as she whipped her head from side to side. Scanning. Searching.

Fear robbed her of breath too fast. Her lungs burned as she grew light-headed. Had anyone else even seen the girl fall? What if Delia was the only one looking for her, and what would happen now that even she'd lost sight of her?

Breaking the surface, she hauled in a giant gulp of air, then forced herself to dive deeper. Legs kicking fast, she felt something tickle her outstretched hand. Forcing her body deeper, she couldn't quite catch the blur of white she spotted in the water through burning eyes.

And then another swimmer streaked past her as if powered by scuba fins. There was a rush of water as strong limbs sluiced by. Though her vision was distorted by the sting of salt, she could tell the new arrival was on target for the flash of white she'd spotted. Even as her chest threatened to explode from lack of air, she remained underwater long enough to be sure the diver retrieved the child.

Thank you, God.

The fear fueling her strokes leaked away. Relief kicked in along with a wave of weariness. By the time she got to the surface, she could barely drag in air, she was so woozy and exhausted, yet she could see through painful eyes as the victim was pulled to safety on the dock.

But now it seemed that Delia was the one in trouble. Gagging, gasping, her arms flailing, she reached blindly for the side of the boat or anything, clawing for support…

"Whoa!" A deep, masculine voice sounded in her ear at the same moment two arms wrapped around her midsection. "I've got you."

Only then did she realize she'd somehow clawed him too. The arm that held her was bleeding from three shallow scratches. Sense slowly returned as oxygen fed her brain again.

The house music had been silenced. The only sound now was the murmur of voices drifting from the marina. She glimpsed the drenched little girl on the dock, already surrounded by family. A woman—a local with a houseboat who happened to be a retired RN—was on her knees at the victim's side, lifting her gently as she coughed up water. The relief in the crowd was palpable. Delia felt the same overwhelming gratitude throughout her body. Her shoulders sagged.

Bringing her breasts into intimate contact with the arm around her. She collapsed like a wet noodle against the slick, hot body of a man built like iron.

Her dress floated like seaweed around her thighs, making her suddenly aware of the way her soaked bikini panties were all that separated her from him.

"Are you okay, Delia?" The voice in her ear was familiar; she'd heard it nearly every day for the past year, even if she hadn't seen the man in person for weeks on end.

Her boss. Jager McNeill.

"Fine," she spluttered, the word ending in a cough.

Of course, it was foolish to be embarrassed since she had dived in the water to save a child. And yet, it still felt terribly awkward to be caught with her dress up around her waist today of all days when she'd wanted to make the perfect professional impression.

Also, she'd scratched him.

Coughed all over him.

If she hadn't had a crush on him once upon a time, maybe she wouldn't be tingling from head to toe right now in spite of everything. But she feared if she tried to swim away from him to escape all the feelings, she just might drown. She was surprised to notice how far she'd drifted from the dock in her search. Behind them, she noticed the transport skiff that Cyril had sent out to meet Jager's seaplane. Jager must have been arriving at the same time she'd jumped into the water.

"Hold onto my shoulders," he told her, shifting their positions in the water so he faced her. "I'll tow you to the dock."

Nose to nose with him, Delia stared up into his

steel-blue eyes. She thought she'd gotten used to his good looks in the past two years that they'd known each other. His dark hair and sharp, shadowed jaw made for enticing contrasts to those incredibly blue eyes. His hair had grown longer in the past months, as if barber visits were the last thing on his mind. But the way the damp strands curled along the strong column of his neck only added to the appeal.

This close, she had the benefit of sensing the wealth of muscle in his athletic body where he held her. Feeling the flush of heat course through her, she ducked deeper into the cold water to hide her reaction to him.

"I can make it." Shaking her head, she scattered droplets from her wet hair. "I just needed to catch my breath."

She attempted to paddle away, but Jager only gripped her tighter.

Oh. My.

Feeling the warmth of his chest through their clingy clothes roused an ache she should not be feeling for her boss. Adding to the problem, the strapless bra she'd been wearing had shifted lower on her rib cage, where it did absolutely no good.

"Humor me," he ordered her, his voice as controlled as his movements. "You're exhausted and dry land is farther away than it looks." He took one of her hands and placed it on his right shoulder. Then, turning away from her, he very deliberately set her other hand on his left shoulder.

He began to swim toward the dock with measured strokes, towing her along behind him. Water lapped over them in light waves. She felt every ripple of his muscles under her palms as the light waves swished over them. She debated fishing one hand down her dress to haul up her bra before they reached land, but decided the potential scolding from Jager if she let go of him wasn't worth it. So she clung to him and gritted her teeth against the friction of her pebbled breasts rubbing against his back. By now he had to be as keenly aware of her as she was of him.

The only positive of this awkward reunion?

Any anxiety she had about talking business with him was utterly eclipsed by physical awareness. So when they reached land, she clamped onto the dock, evenly met his blue gaze and said, "I definitely deserve a raise."

Two hours later, when they were safely back at the McNeill family estate in Le François, Jager still couldn't erase Delia Rickard from his mind. After pouring himself an aged whiskey from the cut crystal decanter on his desk and taking a sip, he stared out his office window through the slats of the open plantation shutters. His gaze kept returning to the guest cottage lit by white landscape lights. He was waiting for Delia to emerge. When he'd first asked her to manage the Martinique household for him, he'd offered her the cottage on the British Colonial style property for expediency's sake.

Not only could she keep track of the staff better on-site, but at the time, she had also been trying to put some distance between herself and her past. Her former fiancé, Brandon Nelson, was a particular kind of son of a bitch Jager had run into often in business—always looking for a way to cheat the system. In this case, the guy had attempted to scam Delia out of her rightful inheritance—a plot of land belonging to her father that was in the way of a proposed landing strip for private aircrafts serving a luxury hotel development. The investors had offered Brandon a cash payment if he could convince her to sign over the rights. He'd decided to simply marry her and obtain the rights for himself.

Unethically.

Jager leaned a hip on the dark hardwood desk, remembering how Delia had discovered the truth on the morning of her wedding. She'd fled the seaside venue on a Jet Ski and run it aground on a small island where Jager had been fishing. It had been the start of a friendship that had benefitted them both.

He'd been in a relationship at the time, and Delia had been running from an awful one, so he'd tamped down the attraction for both of their sakes. Instead, he'd offered her a job. Very quickly, she'd proven an excellent assistant, invaluable in helping him repurpose a portion of the family estate for private parties and occasional corporate retreats as a way to support local businesses—in particular, his marina. After Delia trimmed the household budget the first year and made a local farm-to-table initiative on McNeill lands a success, Jager had asked her to expand her role to review the operations at the marina as well.

Leaving things in her capable hands, he'd moved to California with his brother to take Damon's start-up to the next level. Just thinking about the hell that move had caused for all of them made his shoulders sag with grief for Damon and the loss of his vibrant and beautiful wife.

Now Damon had disappeared too. He'd left to travel two months ago and at the time, Jager had agreed it would be wise for him to get away. But days after his departure, Damon had shut off his phone and hadn't been in contact since.

To make it worse, around that time Jager had been contacted by their father, who'd barely acknowledged him as a child and whom Jager hadn't seen in fifteen years. Now, suddenly, he was offering the help of his wealthy family.

Too little. Too late.

As if Jager had any desire to spend time with the dirtbag who'd walked out on their mom. Apparently Jager's paternal grandfather—whom he'd never met—was determined to reunite all his grandsons. Bastard offspring and otherwise. Jager had told them hell no.

He finished off the whiskey and set aside his glass.

His world was a giant mess. The one moment of clarity in it all?

When Delia had been in his arms in the water just two hours ago. The dark churn of thoughts that had plagued him for nearly a year suddenly quieted, burned away by an attraction grown more intense since that first day when she'd washed up on his island. Nothing prohibited them from being together now. He was so distant from the Martinique-based businesses that he could make a move without worrying about the impact on their working relationship. Or he'd simply transfer her to another part of the company where Gabe could monitor her job performance, eliminating the conflict of interest. Gabe could make the decision about that raise she wanted.

His conscience clear, Jager watched her step from the cottage, her fair hair glowing golden under the porch light as she locked the dead bolt with a key. Now he could allow himself to think about the possibilities of being alone with her. Of forgetting the hell of the past year for a night in her arms.

Backing away from the window, Jager watched as Delia strode toward the main house. She wore a rose-colored tank dress, with a thin white sweater thrown over her shoulders. A simple gold bangle wrapped around one wrist. She worried her lip with her teeth as she stared down at the dusky gold pavers that led to the stone steps up to the house.

If he could have a taste of that soft pink mouth, he would indulge as often as possible. Was she nervous about spending the evening with him? Or was she looking forward to it as much as he? She had to have known she was getting to him today in the water. Soaking wet and hard as hell for her, he'd been unable to hide his fast reaction to feeling her breasts pressed to his chest. He'd felt her reaction too though. The attraction wasn't one-sided.

"Hello, Jager." He couldn't believe how long he'd allowed himself to ruminate over her body. She'd entered the house and his office while he was preoccupied.

Of course, she had domain over the whole place while he was gone. And he'd left the double doors to his office open. He was more than ready to let her in.

"I trust you're feeling better after the impromptu swim?" He turned to greet her but did not approach, hoping to put her at ease. She'd pinned her golden-blond hair up, leaving only a few stray pieces around her face. The rest bounced in a loose knot as she walked.

He gestured toward the seating arrangement near the fireplace. A wrought iron candelabra with fat white pillar candles had been laid in the cold hearth at some point in his absence. A homey touch. Delia perched on the edge of a wide gray twill armchair near the rattan chest that served as a coffee table, her posture stiff even though she gave him a smile.

"I'm almost warm again, thank you." She tugged the shawl sweater more tightly around her while he took a seat on the couch adjacent to her chair. "Tourists may swim in November, but I don't usually go in the water this time of year."

"Yet you didn't even hesitate." He'd been watching her from the deck of the skiff carrying him from the seaplane to the marina. "I saw how fast you jumped in after Emily fell." He'd spoken to the girl's family briefly after reaching the dock, to make sure she was going to be fine and that they would focus more on parenting and less on partying.

"You were in the water almost as quickly as me." She shook her head and briefly closed her hazel eyes as a delicate shudder passed through her. "I don't even want to think about what might have happened if you hadn't arrived when you did. I was never so panicked as those few seconds when I couldn't find her."

"I only spotted her because you were just above her in the water." He'd swum faster than he'd known he was capable of. "Although I would have searched the whole damn marina for her if I had to. I've had enough sleepless nights thinking about how different our lives might be if someone had been there to haul Caroline out of the water."

He hadn't meant to share that, but the loss of his sister-in-law had overshadowed everything else for their family. Delia's hand on his forearm cut through some of the darkness though, providing an unexpected comfort.

"I'm sorry," she said simply, her eyes filled with genuine empathy.

Empathy that didn't even rightfully belong to him. It was Damon who'd been through hell. Suddenly

Jager was reminded that he needed to focus on his family and not whatever he was feeling for his assistant right now. At least until they'd cleared up some business.

"Thank you." He acknowledged her kindness before redirecting the conversation. "Which reminds me that I won't be staying in town long, so I'd like to come up with a plan to review any new business over the next week."

"You're leaving again? Why?" Delia's touch fell away from his arm. Her lips parted in surprise.

"I need to find Damon." He'd never imagined his brother as the kind of man who might do himself harm, but Damon had been through more than any man should have to bear.

"I understand." Delia nodded, but her expression remained troubled. She spun the gold bangle around her wrist.

"I won't leave until we address any concerns you may have about the business." Or Gabe did. But there was enough time to share his plan with her. He still hoped to put her at ease first.

"Of course." She quit spinning the bracelet and glanced up at him. "I know how committed you are to this place. You're always quick to respond to any of my questions about the business."

Leaving him to wonder if she'd ever had questions of a more personal nature that he'd overlooked? He studied her features, trying to read the woman who'd become so adept at managing his affairs. A woman who had become a professional force to be reckoned with despite a lack of formal training.

She deftly changed the subject.

"Have you eaten?" she asked, straightening in her seat. "Dinner is ready. Chef texted me half an hour ago to say he'd prepared something—"

"Will you join me?" he asked, wanting her with him.

"I don't want to monopolize your time on your first day home." She scooted to the edge of her seat as if looking for the closest exit. Cautious. Professional. "I can bring you up to speed on the house and marina in the morning so you can enjoy your meal."

"My brother Gabe is in Los Altos Hills for another week," he reminded her. "There's no one else in Le François waiting to spend time with me, I'm afraid."

Still, she hesitated. No doubt about it, those chilly moments wrapped around one another in the Atlantic today had shifted the dynamic between them. She'd never been uneasy around him before.

"We can make it a working dinner, if you wish." He reached for his phone and began to type out a text. "I'm requesting that the meal be served in here."

"That's not necessary," she protested.

"I insist." He needed them to clear away an important piece of business. To remove any barrier there was to being together. "Besides, I've been meaning to discuss something you brought up in the water today."

"I…" Her eyes went wide. She swallowed visibly.

If she were any other woman, he wouldn't hesitate to end the suspense and kiss her.

But he wouldn't rush this.

"You mentioned needing a raise?" he reminded her, clearing a place for their plates on the rattan chest by moving aside a fresh flower arrangement of spiky red blooms he recognized as native to the island.

Already, a uniformed server hesitated at the office door, a tray in hand. He waved the young woman in.

"Sir?" The woman's starched gray uniform was cinched tight by apron strings. She carefully set the tray down where he indicated. "Chef said to tell you there is a visitor at the gate."

"There is?" Delia tugged her phone out of a long brown leather wallet that she'd deposited on the chair beside her. The call button at the gate on the main road was hooked up to an app Delia and Jager could access. "I'm sorry I didn't hear the bell. I turned off notifications for our meeting."

Curious, Jager spun his own phone toward him and clicked on the icon for the security system while the server went to retrieve another tray from a rolling cart in the hallway.

Before Jager pulled up the video feed from the front gate, Delia gasped.

"What is it?" Jager asked.

She lost color in her face, her fingers hovering above her lips as if to hold in the rest of her reaction.

"It's not your ex, is it?" Jager shot to his feet, moving behind her chair to view her screen.

"No." Delia lifted the phone to show him. "It's your brother. Damon."

Two

Steel-blue eyes stared up into the security camera. McNeill eyes. Delia had seen the three brothers together often enough to appreciate the family resemblance. The striking blue eyes and dark hair. The strong jaw and athletic build. Damon was the tallest of the three. He looked a bit thinner than she recalled, which was no surprise given the year he'd had.

"That's not Damon." The cold harshness of Jager's voice stunned her as he tugged her phone from her grip, his strong hands brushing over her fingers. "Let me speak to him."

Confused, she let go of the device while Jager pressed the talk button. Her skin was still humming from his touch as he straightened.

"I've made it clear I don't want to see anyone from your family," he barked into the speaker while he gently closed the office doors to keep their conversation private from the staff. "If you need accommodations in town, I can send someone out to the gate with a list of recommendations."

"Jager!" Appalled, Delia leaped from her seat and reached to take her phone back. "What are you doing?"

The voice of the man at the gate rumbled through the speaker. "You're not getting rid of us, dude. Now that my grandfather knows about you, the old man is insistent that you and your brothers join the fold."

Delia froze as she absorbed the words. After hearing him speak, she questioned her own eyes. The man didn't have Damon's voice. Or his reserved, deliberate manner. The voice was bolder, more casual, even a bit brash.

Her gaze found Jager's, searching for answers. The air sparked between them, making her realize how close she was standing to her boss. She was painfully aware of how handsome he was in a pair of khakis and a long-sleeved dark tee that showed off his toned body. She caught a hint of his aftershave: pine and musk. Her heartbeat quickened before she stepped back fast.

"Not going to happen, Cam." Jager spoke softly, but there was an edge to his voice she couldn't recall hearing before. Clearly, he knew the man. "You can tell your grandfather that your father made the best possible decision when he walked out on my mother. We're better off without him."

Delia backed up another step, processing. The men looked so much alike. The man at the gate wanted Jager and his brothers to *join the fold* and said his grandfather knew about them now.

The man *was* Jager's brother. Just not the brother that Delia had assumed he was. This was a relation she'd never known about—a half brother.

"We have a lead on Damon," the visitor countered in a more guarded tone. "My brother Ian knows an excellent private investigator—"

"Damon is not your concern," Jager told him shortly, still studying Delia with that watchful gaze. "Goodbye."

He lowered the phone and pressed the button to end the connection and shut down the security app. Sudden silence echoed in Jager's office.

"You have more family than just Damon and Gabriel," she observed, feeling shaken from the encounter. From the whole day that had left her exposed in more ways than one.

It seemed as if Jager had whole facets of his life that she knew nothing about. If he didn't trust her with that information, how well did she even know him? Her former fiancé had left her more than a little wary of men who kept secrets.

"My father was a sporadic part of my childhood at best, and I haven't seen him once since my thirteenth birthday." Jager set her phone on the sofa table next to a platter of food covered with a silver dome.

She'd forgotten about the dinner, but the spices of island cooking—French Creole dishes that were Jager's favorite—scented the air.

"He had other children?" She felt she was owed an answer because of their friendship but she also needed to know about this to do her job. "This can have an impact on all your businesses. You'll want to protect yourself from outside legal claims."

"And so we will." His lips twisted in a wry expression. "But the Manhattan branch of the McNeill family is far wealthier than we can imagine thanks to their global resort empire, so they certainly don't need to alienate their own relatives by forcing their way into our businesses." He gestured to the sofa. "Please sit. We should eat before the meal is cold."

"McNeill Resorts? Oh, wow." The name was as familiar as Hilton. Ritz-Carlton. It was too much to process. She sank down onto the soft twill chair cushion.

Jager took the opportunity to lift the domes from the serving platters and pass her a plate and silverware. The scent of *accras*, the delectable fritters the McNeills' chef made so well, tempted her, rousing an appetite after all.

"Yes. Wow." His tone was biting. "I believe my half brothers expected Gabe and me to swoon when they informed us we were now welcome into the family." He dished out a sampling of the gourmet offerings onto her plate—spiced *chatrou*, the small octopus that was a local delicacy, plus some grilled chicken in an aromatic coconut sauce.

His arm brushed hers. The intimacy of this private meal reminded her she needed to be careful around him. She needed this job desperately. Her father relied on her and good opportunities were difficult to come by locally for a woman with no college degree. She couldn't afford to leave the island to find more options. Balancing her plate carefully, she shifted deeper against the seat cushion to try to insert some space between her and her tempting dining companion.

"Damon doesn't know about them?" she asked, trying to focus her scattered thoughts on his last comment.

"Only in a peripheral way. We were aware of their existence for years, but they didn't contact us until recently." Jager filled his plate as well. "Cameron McNeill and his brother Ian flew out to Los Altos Hills last month to introduce themselves and make it clear their grandfather wants to unite the whole family. Including the bastard Martinique branch."

Delia took her time responding, biting into the tender chicken and taking a sip from the water glass Jager passed her. She knew that he had no love for his father after the man disappeared from their lives—refusing to leave his wife for Jager's mother—when Gabe, the youngest son, was just ten years old. Their father had only visited the boys a few times a year before that, making it impossible to build a relationship. They'd lived in California back then. But after the father quit coming to visit, their mother sold the house and used the proceeds to buy an old plantation home in Martinique, purposely making it difficult for the boys' father to find them even if he'd wanted to. As far as Jager was concerned, however, his father had abandoned their family long before that time.

Jager had shared all that with Delia in the past, but the latest developments were news to her.

"It's the right thing for your grandfather to do," she said finally. "You, Damon and Gabe have as much claim to the McNeill empire as your father's legitimate sons."

"Not in the eyes of the law." Jager scowled down at his plate.

"The business belongs to your grandfather." She knew the rudimentary facts about the hotel giant. They owned enough properties throughout the Caribbean to warrant regular coverage in regional news publications. "Malcolm McNeill gets to choose how he wants to divide his legacy." She waited a moment, and when he didn't argue, she continued, "Have you met him?"

"Absolutely not. That's what they want—for me to get on a plane and go to New York to meet the old man." He speared a piece of white fish with his fork. "They claim Malcolm McNeill is in declining health, but if it's true, they're keeping a tight lock on the news since I haven't seen a whisper of it in the business pages."

Her jaw dropped. How could he be so stubborn?

"Jager, what if something happened to him and you never got to meet him?" She only had her father for family, so she couldn't imagine what it might be like to have more siblings and family who wanted to be a part of her life. "They're family."

"By blood, maybe. But not by any definition that matters in my book." Reaching for a bottle of chilled Viognier the server had left for them, Jager poured two glasses, passing her one before taking a sip of his own.

"And does Gabe feel the same way?" She had a hard time imagining the youngest McNeill digging his heels in so completely. Whereas Jager resolutely watched over his siblings like a de facto father, Gabe went his own way more often than not. He'd only invested in Transparent—Damon's tech company—after considerable urging from his siblings. Gabe preferred to stick close to the hotel he owned on Martinique and was renovating the place by hand.

His older brothers had scoffed at the manual labor, but Delia noticed that Gabe was having a hard time finishing the hotel work because his craftsmanship skills had developed a following, making him in demand for other restoration projects around the Caribbean, all the way to Miami.

"Gabe is outvoted by Damon and me." He took two more bites before he noticed she hadn't responded. When he turned toward her, she glared at him.

"Meaning he disagrees?" she asked.

"Meaning Damon would feel the same way I do, so if Gabe chooses to disagree, he's still outnumbered."

Delia set her plate aside on the rattan chest, then put her wineglass beside it.

"Damon might have a very different opinion about family after losing someone," she observed quietly.

Jager went still.

"You have a lot to say about something that doesn't concern you, Delia." He set aside his half-eaten meal as well, and turned to face her.

"Doesn't it?" She shifted toward him, their knees almost brushing. "I could give you an update on my plans for next year's community garden or how to increase profits at the marina, but it's hard to ignore the fact that you just turned your back on a family member who looks eerily like your missing brother."

"It's not eerie." His tone softened. "It's simple genetics. And I find you a whole lot tougher to ignore than my half brother."

She opened her mouth to deliver a retort and found herself speechless. The air in the room changed—as if the molecules had swollen up with heat and weight, pressing down on her. Making her far too aware of scents, sounds and him.

"That's good," she said finally, recovering herself—barely. She needed to tackle his comment head-on, address whatever simmered between them before they both got burned. “Because I don’t want to be ignored. I would have hoped you’d listen to my opinion the way I once listened to yours when I was having some rough times.”

She hoped that it was safe to remind him of the start to their relationship. She’d felt a flare of attraction for him that day too, but she’d been too shredded by her former fiancé and too mistrusting of her own judgment to act on it. For his part, Jager had seemed oblivious to her eyes wandering over his muscled chest and lean hips covered by a sea-washed pair of swim trunks. He’d quietly assessed the situation despite her tearful outburst about her thwarted marriage, and he’d given her direction, plus a face-saving way out of her dilemma at the time.

She hadn’t been able to pay the taxes on the family’s land that year either. Her dad had been injured in a fishing accident three years ago and couldn’t earn half the living he used to selling fresh catch to local restaurants. But Jager had given her a job and the income had staved off foreclosure. Plus, Jager had given her a place to stay far away from her ex, and time to find herself.

Now, he looked at her with warmth in his blue eyes. A heat that might stem from something more than friendship.

“Maybe I liked to flatter myself that I was the one doling out all the advice in this relationship.” His self-deprecating smile slid past her defenses faster than any heated touch.

"I don't think any of us exercise our best judgment when our world is flipped upside down." She'd been a wreck when they'd met. Literally. She'd almost plowed right into him on a Jet Ski she'd taken from the dock near where she'd planned to say her vows.

"Is that what's happening here?" he asked, shifting on the sofa cushions in a way that squared them up somehow. Put him fractionally closer. "The world is off-kilter today?"

The low rasp of his voice, a subtle intimacy of tone that she hadn't heard from him before, brought heat raining down over her skin. Her gaze lowered to his mouth before she thought the better of it.

"That's not what I meant." She felt breathless. Her words were a light whisper of air, but she couldn't draw a deep breath without inhaling the scent of him.

Without wanting him.

"It's true though." He skimmed a touch just below her chin, drawing her eyes up to his. "Something happened in the water today. Something changed between us."

No, she wanted to protest. To call it out for a lie.

Yet he was right and they both knew it.

His touch lingered, the barest brush of his knuckles beneath her jaw. She wanted to dip her cheek toward his hand to increase the pressure, to really feel him.

Madness. Total madness to think it, let alone act on it.

"We can't let that happen." She needed to maintain the balance of power. Rebuild some guise of professionalism before it was too late. "This job is too important to me."

Shakily, she shot to her feet. She stalked to the window on legs that felt like liquid, forcing herself to focus. To get this conversation back on track. Why hadn't she simply spoken to him about the community garden?

"And your professional skills are valuable to me as well. But we can work around that." Behind her, his voice was controlled. Far more level than she felt. "Besides, do you really believe ignoring it will make it go away, Delia?"

She felt him approach, his step quiet but certain. He stood beside her at the window, giving her personal space, yet not conceding her point. The soft glow of a nearby sconce cast his face in partial shadow.

"If we both make an effort, yes. Of course." She nodded, hoping she sounded more sure of herself than she felt. "We're both adults with professional agendas. We can keep those work goals front and center when we're together."

"Like we did today." His gaze fixed on some point outside the window, but his eyebrows rose in question.

"Today was an aberration." It had to be. "Emotions ran high. We were both scared for Emily." She wanted it to be as simple as that. "Just an adrenaline moment."

Her heart fluttered oddly as he turned toward her again, taking her measure. Seeing right through her.

"So what about this moment, right now?" he asked. "Adrenaline?"

She licked her suddenly-dry lips. Willed herself to come up with a logical explanation for the way the air simmered all around them. The way her skin sensed his every movement.

Any answer she might have given was a moot point, however, since Jager chose that moment to lower his lips to hers.

Jager couldn't walk away from her tonight. Not after the hellish year he'd had. He needed this. Needed her.

Her lips were softer than any woman's he'd ever tasted. She kissed with a tentative hunger—gentle and curious, questing and cautious at the same time. She swayed near him for a moment, her slender body as pliable as it had been in the water today, moving where he guided her. So he slid his hands around her waist, dipping them beneath the lightweight cotton sweater to rest on the indent just above her hips.

She felt as good as she tasted. Something buzzed loudly in his brain—a warning, maybe, telling him to take it slower. But he couldn't do a damned thing to stop it.

Instead, he gripped the fabric of her dress in his hands, a tactic to keep from gripping her too hard. He tugged the knit material toward him, drawing her more fully against him.

Yes.

Her breasts were as delectable as he remembered from in the water today. High. Firm. Perfect. And Delia seemed to lose herself in the contact as much as he. She looped her arms around his neck, pressing her whole body to his in a way that made flames leap inside him. Heat licked over his skin, singeing him. Making him realize how cold he'd been inside for months.

Delia's kiss burned all that away. Torched everything else but this incredible connection. The warning buzz in his brain short-circuited and finally shut the hell up.

Letting go of her dress, he splayed his fingers on the curve of her ass, drawing her hips fully to his. The soft moan in her throat sounded like approval, but he was so hungry for her he didn't trust what he heard.

"Delia." He broke the kiss and angled back to see her better, trying to blink through the fog of desire. "I want you. Here. Now."

"Yes. Yes." She said it over and over, a whispered chant as if to hurry him along, her hands restlessly trolling his chest, slipping beneath his shirt. "Definitely now. If you lock the doors," she suggested right before she lowered a kiss to his shoulder, "I can get the blinds."

"I'm not letting you go for even a second." He walked her backward toward the door, kissing her most of the way until he needed to focus on the bolt. Even then, he kept one palm on her lower back, at the base of her dress's zipper.

"And the blinds?" she reminded him, her hair starting to fall from the topknot she was wearing. "The switch on your desk is closest."

"Right. Of course. Lady, you do mess with my brain." His brain—and other parts of him.

Jager moved with her in that direction, but he used his free hand to sift through her silky hair, pulling out pins and one jeweled comb, letting them fall to the dark bamboo floor. He'd been wanting to do this forever, he realized. Ever since he'd held her that first day when she wore that wet wedding gown and cried her eyes out against his bare chest.

She reached to find the switch, lowering the blinds electronically, shutting the room off from the well-lit grounds. Now just a few low lamps illuminated his office, casting appealing shadows on her creamy pale skin. With her tousled hair falling over one eye and the shadows slanting over her, she looked decidedly wanton. Altogether appealing.

He wanted her so much his teeth ached. He tugged the zipper down on her dress, peeling the cotton knit away from her body, sliding it right off her shoulders to pool at narrow hips. One quick shimmy and she kicked free of the dress; now she was clad only in ice-blue satin panties and a matching strapless bra. She was even more beautiful than he'd imagined, and he'd had some dreams where he'd thoroughly fantasized about her over the past two years.

Before he could contemplate how best to savor her, she slid a finger between her breasts and loosened the tiny clasp of her bra, baring herself. He froze for an instant to take in the sight of her—then his body unleashed into motion. His arms were already moving as he hauled off his shirt so he could feel her against him.

Kissing her, he cupped her breasts in his hands, teased one taut peak and then the other. Licking, nipping, drawing her deep into his mouth. He backed her into the desk and then lifted her, settling her there. She wrapped her legs around his waist, hooking her ankles and keeping him close.

"Do you have...protection?" she asked, her breath a warm huff of air against his shoulder.

Hell, yes. He might not have been with anyone in months, but he always kept a supply of condoms here. Pulling away, he opened the middle desk drawer. Thumbed past the last file. Emerged with a packet.

Their eyes met over the condom before she plucked it from his fingers and kissed him. No hesitation. No reservations.

He tunneled his hands through her hair, tilting her head back to taste his way along her jaw and behind one ear. She shivered sweetly against him, deliciously responsive. She smelled sweet there, like vanilla. He lingered, inhaling her, relishing the way her breath caught.

Too soon, her touch along his belt, the backs of her knuckles grazing his erection through his fly, called his attention from her delicate neck. Later, he would return to her neck, he promised himself. He wanted to linger over every part of her, but right now, the need was too fierce to ignore. While he unfastened the belt and carefully freed himself from the zipper, Delia was already tearing open the condom packet, her fingers unsteady as she rolled it into place. Her palm stroking over him there sent a fire roaring inside. He touched her through the blue satin panties she still wore, and he found the hidden dampness just inside and teased a throaty moan from her, stilling her questing hands long enough to let him catch his breath.

He wanted her ready for him. Really ready. Sinking a finger inside her, he felt the deep shudders of her release and kissed her moans quiet as she rode out the storm of sensation.

Damn, but she was beautiful. Her cheeks were flushed and eyes dazed, her hair a golden banner in the low lamplight.

When she was still again, he eased inside her slowly, gripping her thighs with his hands to guide himself home. She wound her arms around him again, nipping his lower lip before drawing it between hers. She arched against him, her breasts flattening to his chest. He knew he wouldn't last long this time. The day had stolen his restraint long before he started peeling her clothes off.

So he let himself just feel the slick heat of her body around his, her warm vanilla scent making his mouth water for a fuller taste. He cupped one breast and feasted on the taut nipple, finding a rhythm that pleased them both and riding it to…

Heaven.

His release crashed through him, trampling his body like a rogue wave until he could only hold on to Delia. He buried his face in her hair, the shudders moving up his back again and again. Her nails bit pleasantly into his shoulders and he welcomed the sweet hurt to bring him back to earth. Back to reality.

A reality that felt…off, somehow.

Straightening with Delia still in his arms, his body tensed.

"What is it?" The sultry note in her voice told him she hadn't realized what happened yet.

His satiated body was only beginning to get the message too, but his brain had already figured out what was wrong.

"It broke."

Three

Delia's brain didn't compute.

Her limbs still tingled pleasantly from the first orgasm a man had ever given her. Her whole body hummed with sensual fulfillment. And yet…panic was just starting to flood through her nervous system, rattling her from the inside out.

"What do you mean, *it broke*?" She knew what he meant, of course. But she didn't understand how it had happened. How she could have let herself be so carried away by the man and the moment. Even if the man in question was Jager McNeill.

"I don't suppose you're on the pill?" he asked, instead of answering her question, as he gently extricated himself from her arms and legs.

"No." She shook her head while reality slowly chilled the residual heat right out of her veins.

"You should stand up," he urged her, lifting her off the desk and settling her on her feet. "Do you mind if I carry you into the shower?"

His matter-of-fact response to a potential grenade in both their lives only rattled her further, making the possible consequences feel all the more real. And frightening.

"I'll walk there," she assured him, wondering what the rest of his staff—her coworkers, for crying out loud—were going to think of her walk of shame through his house into the nearest bathroom.

She would headline local gossip for weeks. Or, quite possibly, nine months.

Oh, God. What had she done?

"We could try emergency contraception," Jager suggested carefully. "If you're amenable to taking the medication."

Would that work? She'd never had a need to investigate the option. "I can call my doctor."

Jager was putting a blanket around her. The throw from the back of the couch, she realized. Gratefully, she sank into the gray cashmere, veiling her tender body from the cool calculation she now saw in her lover's eyes. He'd pulled on his pants and shrugged into his long-sleeved black shirt. Only his dark hair, disheveled from her fingers, gave away the less guarded man who'd made passionate love to her just moments ago.

Not that it was love, she reminded herself sharply.

"I'm sure I can find a pharmacy with the over-the-counter variety." Jager was all efficiency. "I'll get you settled and make a trip to the store."

"Thank you." She would still want to talk to her doctor. Double-check the side effects given her medical history. But she wasn't sure how much to disclose about that right now with her thoughts churning.

"The guest room is closest," he told her, tucking her under one strong arm as he opened the double doors of his office and steered her into the hallway.

Of course she knew the guest room was closest. She'd been in this house every day for two years. Would she lose her job now if she was carrying his child? Or even if she wasn't? Only pride kept her from blurting out how much she needed this job.

When they arrived in the downstairs guest suite, Jager locked the door behind him and she scurried toward the bathroom.

"Delia." His voice halted her just before she shut the door behind her.

Peeking out through a crack—not that it mattered since he'd already seen her very naked—she waited to see what he wanted. And wished she saw some hint of warmth in his eyes to reassure her.

"I believe emergency contraception has a high rate of effectiveness. But based on where you are in your cycle, how strong of a chance would there be that this would have—" He hesitated, and she wondered if this was rattling him more than he let on.

But he blinked, and any hint of uncertainty vanished. "Resulted in pregnancy?"

"Based solely on my cycle?" She had no idea if she was a fertile woman. But if so? "We would want to come up with a contingency plan when I get out of the shower."

Delia felt marginally calmer when she emerged from the bathroom in a pair of navy cotton shorts and a tee with McNeill Meadows printed on one pocket—promotional items given away to school groups who visited the community garden. She'd found a stack of clean items still in the packaging in the back of the guest bathroom's linen closet. Indulging herself, she'd helped herself to two tees to make up for the fact that her bra still lay on the floor of Jager's office.

She used a hand towel to dry her hair a bit more as she padded across the thick Persian carpet toward the king-size bed with its pristine white duvet. This bedroom overlooked the gardens, its deep balcony almost as large as the room itself. The sliding glass pocket doors were open now, and she followed the floral-scented breeze to where Jager sat on a padded chaise longue, looking out at the lit paths of the rock garden. The table nearby was set for two, a hurricane lamp glowing between the place settings of all white dishes. New serving platters undoubtedly held an entirely new meal. Sandwiches, maybe. Or fruit and cheese. Not even the McNeills' talented chef could turn out five-star cuisine on an hourly basis.

The travertine tiles were cold on her bare feet as she padded outside to join Jager. He turned when she'd almost reached him, then stood.

"Would you be more comfortable in your own clothes?" he asked. "I brought them from the office and put your things in the closet."

She winced to think of her wrinkled dress neatly hung in one of the gargantuan closets. "No, thank you. I've always liked these McNeill Meadows tees. I chose them last year for when school groups visit. At long last, I'll have my own."

"You wear it well." His blue gaze slid over her and she felt it as keenly as any touch. "I had some food brought up in case you're hungry. I wasn't much of a host the first time around."

Her stomach rumbled an answer at the same time she nodded. Needing to stay cool and levelheaded, she focused on slow, calming breaths. She draped the damp hand towel over one of the stone railings surrounding the balcony, then let him lead her to the table. The outdoor carpet was warm against her bare toes. He held out a chair for her and she sank into the wide seat. Once he tucked her chair in, he opened the platters, offering her each so she could help herself to a selection of fruits, cheeses and warm baguettes. Jager poured them both glasses of sparkling water over ice and lemons, then sat in the seat beside her. The hurricane lamp sent gold light flickering over the table while night birds called in the trees just off the balcony.

To a bystander, it would look like the perfect romantic setting. She guessed romance couldn't be further from either of their minds.

"Based on your comment going into the shower earlier, I thought it would be wise to discuss a plan for the future. Just in case." He slid a paper bag across the table. "Although I was able to obtain the contraception option we discussed."

She eyed the bag dubiously, but took it after a moment. "I'd like to check with my own doctor in the morning, but if he gives me the okay, I'll take it then."

"That sounds fair." He nodded.

"Thank you." She congratulated herself on her calm tone that belied the wild knot of fears in her belly. She focused on her wedge of brie, spreading the cheese on a thin slice of baguette.

Jager laid a hand on her knee, an intimacy she hadn't expected after how quickly he'd pulled away following the encounter in his office. It felt good. Too good. She couldn't allow herself to fall for him. One moment of passionate madness was one too many when she needed this job and the good will of the McNeills to help keep the Rickard home and land.

"Let me begin by assuring you that I would never abandon my child." Jager spoke with a fierceness that gave her pause. "My father taught me well the damage a parent inflicts with his absence."

The candle flame leaped and the glow was reflected in his eyes. She wasn't sure how to interpret his words, however.

"Neither would I," she told him evenly. Family loyalty meant everything to her. Her father had raised her by himself, on the most meager means, after losing his wife in childbirth.

Some of the intensity faded from Jager's expression. He lifted his hand from her knee and sipped his water before replacing the glass on the white linen tablecloth.

"Then we'll have to stick together if tonight has consequences," Jager observed. "In the meantime, I think I should fly out as soon as possible to begin the search for my brother. I want to find Damon so I can return here next month or in six weeks, whenever you think we might learn one way or another about a possible pregnancy."

Her knife clattered to her plate as she lost her grip. She fumbled to retrieve it, but couldn't hide her dismay at his quick abandonment. "I have set a new record for chasing a man out of my bed." Resentment stirred. "I can email you the test results, if it comes down to that."

"Delia." He set down his own cutlery to reach across the table, his hand circling one of her wrists. "It never occurred to me you might want to travel with me, but I can arrange for that. Our chemistry is undeniable."

Defensiveness prickled. She wasn't planning to be his mistress.

"What about my job? I need the work, Jager. My father relies on my income. That's why I asked about the raise before things got…complicated."

"I had already planned to ask Gabe to supervise your work from now on. To eliminate any conflict of interest for me. But in light of what's happened—"

"You already had a plan in place to have an *affair* and didn't tell me?" She wondered when he'd decided that. Or when he would have clued her in to the fact. It might have put her more at ease about being with him.

Then again, what did it say about the beginnings of a relationship between them when he made all the decisions?

"I wanted to be with you, Delia." His jaw flexed as he spoke and she had a memory of kissing him there. "I knew it in the water today that we weren't going to be able to continue a productive working relationship with so much tension between us."

She worried her lip, unsure how she felt about that. What if she didn't like working with Gabe? More to the point, what if Gabe didn't need her? If she was pregnant as a result of this night, how could she possibly maintain any independence when she worked for the family of her child's father?

Most important of all? She wasn't sure how she felt about an affair with Jager. Of course she was tempted. She couldn't deny their time together had been incredible. One touch from him and she'd been lost, swamped by a desire so heated she'd forgotten her common sense. But she had a few obvious reservations straight out of the gate.

"I'm not sure we can have a productive personal relationship either if we're not equal partners. I'd like to be a part of the decision-making." She nibbled a strawberry, hungry despite the anxiety.

"I agree," he surprised her by saying. But then, was he just trying to pacify her? "If there's any chance we need to parent together, we'll have to figure out how to share that responsibility in a healthy way."

Determined to at least appear calm and in control, Delia lifted her glass in a silent toast. "We're making progress then. I appreciate you hearing my opinions."

"I value your input. Would you really want to travel with me for the next few weeks? The last I knew, Damon was in Marrakesh."

She took a deep breath, steeling herself for a conversation he wouldn't want to have. But he said he'd share the decision-making power. She didn't plan on accepting his offer to extend this affair if he didn't mean it.

"Your half brother said he knows where Damon is," she reminded him. "On the off chance that it's true, shouldn't you find him as quickly as possible in case he needs you?"

Jager's shoulders tensed. "You're going to make this about my family?"

"Isn't this whole conversation about the possibility of more family? A McNeill child?" Straightening in her seat, she tried to maintain some composure, but she could see him pulling away fast. It was in his shuttered expression.

"I know Damon. That means I can locate him faster than anyone else." He'd sidestepped her question, she noticed. "The only thing left to decide now is if you want to join me in my search, or if you prefer to wait in Le François until we find out for certain if there will be another McNeill in our future?"

Four

Pacing the floor of the cottage bedroom, Delia paused to check her desk calendar for the third time, making sure her dates were right while she waited for the results of the at-home pregnancy test.

The calendar told her the same thing it had before. It was now two weeks until Christmas, and almost six weeks after that fateful night when she'd let her attraction to Jager run wild.

Nearly six weeks since she'd had unprotected sex with her boss, and no sign of her period. She'd ended up taking the morning-after contraception Jager had purchased for her after speaking to her physician, so she'd honestly thought they'd be in the clear, even though she hadn't been able to take the pill within the first twenty-four hours as would have been ideal. But it was still supposed to be highly effective within the first seventy-two hours, so she hadn't panicked when her doctor hadn't gotten back to her personally until the next day.

Still, she'd delayed this test, fearing a false negative result. Better to wait longer and be certain, even if Jager had been texting her daily from Morocco, asking her for updates, tactfully suggesting a blood test at an appointment he'd helpfully arranged. She'd been ducking his calls, which was totally unprofessional given that he still had some sway over her job, despite Gabriel McNeill now technically being the one signing her paycheck. But the longer she went missing her expected period, the more her anxiety spiked.

Because honestly, she was scared to know the truth.

In Jager's last text, he'd informed her he would fly home tonight, insisting they find out for certain one way or another. Knowing she couldn't handle discovering the result in front of him, she'd surrendered and pulled out one of the pregnancy tests she'd purchased two weeks before.

Now she just had to wait three minutes.

Thirty more seconds, she corrected herself after checking her watch. Skin still damp from her bath, Delia tightened the bathrobe tie around her waist and returned to the steamy bathroom where the garden tub was draining. The clove-and-cinnamon-scented bubble bath, which she made from her own recipe during the holidays, was a small decadence she allowed herself at times like this.

The pregnancy test lay facedown on the white tile countertop beside the sink. She'd left it there while she reread the instructions to be sure she understood. One line meant not pregnant. Two lines—however faint—meant she was going to have a child with Jager McNeill.

She'd read online that high tension and stress could delay a period. That *had* to be why she was late. So, holding her breath, she closed her eyes. Flipped over the stick on the cool tile.

Two. Lines.

One bright pink. One paler pink.

There was no denying it. And according to the package, this was the most reliable at-home pregnancy detection kit.

"Oh, no. No." Her legs turned to jelly beneath her. She felt so dizzy she clutched the narrow countertop with both hands to steady herself. The stack of rolled yellow hand towels swayed against the wall as she stared at it.

No, wait. That was her swaying.

She stumbled back to sit on the edge of the garden tub, the last of her bubble bath gurgling down the drain with a sucking swish. Kind of like all the plans she'd had for independence once she had her father more securely settled. Plans to get a college degree one day. To travel somewhere beyond this tiny island where she'd been born.

Plans for a future where she called the shots and dictated her own life. She must not have taken the morning-after medicine soon enough, but at the time, she'd really wanted her doctor's advice about the pill considering her health history.

Wasn't it enough that she'd screwed up by nearly marrying a guy who didn't care about her? Nope. She had to compound her foolishness by succumbing to a moment of passion with a man who would never see her as more than…what? A company employee? A former friend turned sometime lover?

Her child deserved better than that.

That simple truth helped her emotions to level out. Made the dizzy feeling subside a bit. She couldn't afford to wallow in a pity party for what she'd wanted in life. She was going to be a mother, and that was something tremendously significant.

She might have messed up plenty of times on her own behalf, but Delia Rickard was not going to be the kind of woman who made mistakes where her baby was concerned. That didn't mean she had a clue what to do next, but she sure planned to take her time and figure it out.

Deep breath in.

Deep breath out.

Before she even finished the exhale, however, a swift, hard knock sounded on the front door of the cottage.

"Delia?" The deep rumble of the familiar voice caused panic to stab through her.

Jager McNeill had come home.

Jager stood under the cottage porch light, waiting. He knew Delia was here. His housekeeper had seen her enter the carriage house an hour ago and Delia's lights were all on. Soft holiday music played inside.

She'd been avoiding any real conversations with him for weeks. He'd tried to give her some space, knowing she was even more rattled about the possibility of being pregnant than he was. Besides, the search for his brother had been intense, leading him on a circuitous path around the globe. Now he was certain, at least, that Damon was alive. But he'd seen signs that his brother was hell-bent on revenge and that scared him.

Still, Jager should have made Delia his first priority before now. Either she was delaying taking the pregnancy test for reasons he didn't understand or—worse—she'd been hiding the news from him. Whatever the truth, he needed to earn her trust. He couldn't afford to alienate her when their futures might be irrevocably bound.

He lifted his hand to knock again, only to hear the deadbolt slide free on the other side. The doorknob turned and there she was.

Delia.

Wearing a white terry-cloth robe and a pair of red-and-green-striped knee socks, she was scrubbed clean, her wet hair falling in dark gold waves onto her shoulders. Worry filled her hazel eyes. The rosy color he'd grown used to seeing was missing in her cheeks.

Hell.

He hadn't seen her look so upset since that first day they'd met. And that comparison put his own behavior into perspective. He wasn't a loser like her former fiancé. He should have come home before now. Been there for her.

"May I come in?" He hadn't even changed his clothes when he stepped off the plane. He'd flown eight hours to be here today, the six-week anniversary of the passionate encounter in his office.

Six weeks hadn't dimmed how much he wanted her. Not even when they were both stressed and worried about the future. If he had his way, she'd be in his arms already, but he didn't want to pressure her.

"That would be wise." Nodding, Delia retreated while he stepped over the threshold, closing the door behind him.

He hadn't been inside the cottage for over a year. He'd overseen the delivery of a few basic pieces of furniture when she'd first taken up residence in the renovated carriage house. But it bore no resemblance to what he remembered.

To say she painted flowers on the walls didn't come close to describing the way she'd made the interior look like an enchanted garden. Yes, there were flowers of all colors and varieties—some not found in nature—growing from a painted grass border along the floor. On one wall, a full moon glowed in white phosphorescent paint, shining down on a garden path full of rabbits and hedgehogs, all following a girl in a dark blue dress. On another wall, there was a painted mouse hole on the baseboard, with a mouse with a broom and apron beside it, as if the tiny creature had just swept her front mat. Above the couch, framing a window overlooking the garden, someone had painted an elaborate stained-glass frame, as if the window view itself was a painting. The white curtains were drawn and a holiday wreath hung from the curtain rod on a bright red ribbon. He could only imagine the effect in the daytime.

From the living room, Jager spied her small bedroom; a white queen-size bed dominated the space. A canopy made of willow branches around the headboard was covered in white fairy lights that made the whole room glow. The unexpected glimpse into Delia's private space was so distracting that for a moment he'd forgotten his purpose.

"I took the test," Delia announced, passing him a white plastic stick. "Two pink lines. I'm pregnant."

She collapsed down onto the narrow white love seat, her robe billowing out at her sides. Her head dropped into her hands, and she planted her elbows on the bare knees visible just above her knee socks.

For his part, Jager felt like he'd just taken a roundhouse kick to the solar plexus. He'd tried to mentally prepare himself for this outcome for the past six weeks, but he hadn't come close to doing an adequate job.

"You're pregnant." He stared blindly at the two pink lines for a moment before setting the test aside on a glass-topped wrought iron coffee table. He needed to focus on Delia.

Lowering himself to the love seat beside her, he placed a hand on the center of her back, hoping to reassure her. Or maybe himself. He wasn't feeling too steady either.

"I only just found out." She lifted her head from her hands. Her eyes were rimmed with red but there were no tears. "I should have taken the test weeks ago, but I was scared of a false reading. I knew I just wasn't ready for the relief of getting a negative result, only to find out three days later that it hadn't been accurate."

"It's okay." He rubbed circles on her back, trying to remember the to-do list he'd typed into his phone for just this scenario. "I was worried you've known all week and couldn't figure out how to tell me."

"No." She shook her head, damp gold strands of hair clinging to one cheek. "When you texted that you were coming home tonight, I knew I couldn't wait any longer. Bottom line, I've probably been delaying just because I was worried."

"That's why I wanted to be here for you when you found out," he reminded her, wondering how they were going to come to any agreement about the future of their child when they couldn't coordinate something so simple. “I wish you would have responded to my messages.”

A determined expression appeared in her eyes. “I hope you can appreciate that we’re going to have a new dynamic between us now and I can’t be expected to have a sixty-minute window to respond to your texts. You ensured we wouldn’t be working together when you handed over my performance reviews to your brother.”

Surprised at her response, Jager realized there were many facets to this woman that he knew nothing about. Her whimsical love of gardens for one. And this steely, willful side that he’d never suspected lurked beneath her cooperative professional demeanor.

“I never said you needed to reply to my texts within the hour,” he answered, his hand going still on her shoulders where he’d been touching her.

“Perhaps not, but it’s a level of responsiveness I prided myself on when I was your assistant.” She suddenly shot up off the cushions to pace about the small living area, her stocking feet silent on the moss-colored area rug. “Maybe you never noticed, Jager, but not once in two years was I delinquent with a reply.”

He supposed that could be accurate. In truth, he’d never taken that much note. He tucked aside the information to consider later, once they’d gotten through the emotionally charged moment. For now, he focused on remembering the items on the checklist from his phone.

"Fair enough. I realize our relationship has changed radically in a short amount of time. We'll find our way forward together." He kept his tone gentle, unwilling to upset her any more than she already seemed. "I hope you'll agree our next step is a doctor's appointment to confirm the result of your test and ensure you're off to a healthy start."

She stopped her agitated pacing and stared at him blankly for a moment before she resumed.

"Of course." She nodded, but she appeared distracted. She paused beside her wireless speaker and flicked it off, quieting the classical Christmas music. "I'll call my doctor first thing in the morning."

"I'd like to go with you."

She stopped again, her gaze wary. "Why?"

Frustration ground through him at the realization that she could shut him out at any time. Sure, once the child was born he had a way to exercise legal rights. But until then, she could cut him out of a large part of the baby's life—ultrasounds, heartbeats—things he wanted to be a part of. The lack of control in this situation was alien to him.

"To be a part of the process, Delia. I've tried to give you the space you craved these last six weeks." It was tough even now staying in his seat while she paced the floor. He wanted to pull her against him, hold her and remind her how good they could be together in the most fundamental way, but he knew it wasn't the time. "This child is every bit as much my responsibility as yours. I tried to explain to you on the night we made this baby that I will take this duty very seriously." Jager would not be the kind of father Liam McNeill had been.

"Okay." Delia nodded, then bit her lip. "I should warn you though, there's a bit of medical history I'll be sharing at that time. I'm not necessarily worried, but in the interest of taking every precaution—" she hesitated, her fingers massaging her temple gently before she continued "—my own mother died in childbirth."

The revelation speared through him hard. "I should have remembered." She'd shared that with him once, long ago. He tried to recall what little he knew about her past and her family. "You said she went into labor early, while she was out sailing with your father."

He'd met Pascal Rickard once, a stern-faced fisherman who'd stared down Jager when he'd visited Delia's home village to collect some of her things. Jager hadn't wanted her to return home alone after the incident with her ex. Pascal had been in his seventies then, but even with his weathered face, gray hair and half an arm amputated, he'd been an imposing figure. His broad shoulders and burly muscles attested to the hard work he'd done all his life. The man had little to say to his only child when Delia had packed up her small room for good.

"They were having me late in life. My father was

fifty at the time, and my mom was forty-two." Delia hugged her arms around her waist; there was a new level of anguish in the story now that she was going to be a mother too. "Her uterus ruptured. The doctors told my dad afterward there was nothing he could have done to save her. She would have been in critical danger even if she'd been close to a hospital at the time."

The thought of something like that happening to Delia floored Jager. No matter what happened between them romantically, she had been more than just an assistant to him these last two years. Even though they'd seen little of each other these last several months, he considered her a friend.

"Did her doctors know she was at risk?" He would spare no expense to keep Delia safe. He would call specialists. Hire extra help if she needed rest. His mental to-do list grew exponentially.

"She would have been considered high-risk anyway because of her age, but I'm not sure what caused the rupture." Delia swiped a hand through her damp hair, pulling it away from her neck. "Talking about my mother—and particularly my birth—always left my father sad, so I avoided the topic in the past. But now that the events are extremely relevant to me, I will visit him as soon as possible and find out everything I can about what happened."

"I'll drive you there." Jager would clear his schedule and look into hiring someone to follow up on the lead he had to find Damon. Until he knew more about Delia's condition, he wasn't leaving her side.

"I'll be fine." She shook her head, waving away the offer.

"I insist." He rose to his feet, needing to make it clear that he was involved with this pregnancy and staying that way. He closed the distance between them. He didn't reach for her the way he wanted to, but he stood close enough to catch a hint of cinnamon and cloves.

She smelled good enough to eat, reminding him of how long it had been since he'd tasted her. Touched her. He planned to pursue her again as soon as she had the all clear from her doctor.

"Jager, I understand you want to be a part of this, but I won't compromise my independence." Frowning, she huffed out an impatient sigh.

"Giving you a ride is hardly taking away your independence. You can drive us in the Hummer if it makes you feel more in control." He didn't use the huge SUV often, but the vehicle had just the right amount of metal to keep her safe. Delia had driven it before.

"This isn't about who's in the driver's seat." Her chin tilted up. She was stubborn. Fierce. "It's about sharing decision-making. Remember we discussed that? If we're going to be effective co-parents, we need to find a way to share responsibility."

"I remember very well." He couldn't help but feel

stubborn on this subject as well, damn it. Raising a child together was too important.

Which brought him to the second item on his list, every bit as important as the doctor visit.

And even more likely to put that wary look in her eyes.

"Since we want to share responsibility, I suggest we approach co-parenting through the time-honored legal channel that gives us equal rights in the eyes of the law."

He lifted her left hand in his and held it tight. Her gaze followed the movement, brows knitting together in confusion. As he bent over her left hand, he kissed the back of her knuckles. When he straightened, her lips had formed a silent O of surprise. But he didn't even hesitate.

"Delia Rickard, will you marry me?"

Five

Was he serious?

Delia studied Jager's handsome face, trying to understand his motive. He had to know how fiercely she would resist that kind of bloodless arrangement, especially now that she'd had a glimpse of what real passion felt like. She wasn't going to accept anything less than true love if she ever returned to the altar again.

"How can you ask me that after what I went through with my engagement?" Delia slid her fingers free of Jager's hand. Though her skin tingled pleasantly from the contact, her brain rejected his matter-of-fact proposal. She needed time to process all of this. Rushing headlong to make another mistake was not the answer, and she felt like she was hanging on by an emotional thread right now. "I already had one man try to marry me for purely business reasons."

"Our child is hardly a business reason," Jager reminded her. She noticed how he was still wearing his travel clothes: dark jeans, white tee and simply cut black jacket.

She would bet he'd driven here directly from the airport. His face was rough with a few days' whiskers too, making her wonder what his trip chasing Damon around the globe had been like.

"A legal reason then," she told him flatly. "I believe that's the very language you used when you tendered the offer. Marriage as a *legal channel* to raise our child jointly."

He drew a breath, no doubt to launch a counteroffensive, but she was simply not ready for this conversation tonight. His presence already loomed too big in her small living room, and with his child literally growing inside her, it was simply too much.

"Jager, I'm sorry." She stepped closer, hoping to appeal to him as a friend. "I'm still reeling from all of this. Since we'll be spending time together tomorrow to speak to my father and visit the doctor, maybe we could table this discussion for tonight to give us both a chance to get a handle on it?"

"I understand." He nodded but made no move to leave. His blue gaze skimmed over her. "Will you join me for dinner? We can unwind and relax. No need to talk about anything you don't wish to discuss."

She hesitated. And in the small span of silence, he picked up her hand and slid his thumb across the center of her palm in a touch that was deliberately provocative. Or maybe she was just especially sensitive to his caress.

Either way, it gave her shivers.

"Delia, we were together the last time I was here for a reason." His voice wound around her senses, drawing her in. "There is no need to deny ourselves a connection we couldn't resist then either."

She swayed in limbo, hovering between wanting to lose herself in his touch, and wanting to set new parameters for a relationship grown way too complicated. In the end, she wasn't ready to do either. Taking a deep breath, she extricated her fingers from his.

"That connection caused me to make a reckless decision that I'm unwilling to repeat."

Yet.

She knew resisting the pull of Jager McNeill was going to be a Herculean task, but for the sake of their child, she needed to sort out her feelings and make a plan before she ran headlong into another unwise decision.

"Very well." He tipped his head in the barest concession of her point. "I'll wait to hear from you in the morning. Let me know what time to pick you up."

"Thank you. I'll text you." She knew tomorrow she'd face the same temptations all over again—to simply fall back into a heated relationship with Jager and indulge herself. But maybe after a good night's sleep, she'd feel stronger. More ready to think about what kind of preparations she needed to make for her child's future.

"Until then, I hope you bear in mind that I'm sleeping close by and I'm here for you, Delia." He reached out and ran his finger along a damp strand of hair, tucking it behind her ear. Then, lowering his voice, he brushed the back of his knuckles along her cheek. "Day or night."

She felt the sexy promise low in her belly, where desire pooled, thick and hot. All at once, she was reminded of how very naked she was beneath her robe. Of how easy it would be to shrug her way out of it and take the pleasure Jager's touch offered.

For a moment, she didn't dare to breathe, her whole body weak with longing. She guessed that he knew. His blue eyes turned a molten shade for a moment, before he allowed his touch to fall away.

When he departed, bidding her good-night before he closed her door behind him, Delia slumped onto the sofa, her heart beating wildly. Resisting her former boss wasn't going to be easy. How long would he hold back because she asked him to? Another day? A week?

Because she knew with certainty that she would have lost herself in him all over again tonight if he'd pressed his advantage and used all that chemistry to woo her. That meant she needed to be smart. Strong. Resolute.

She couldn't possibly invite Jager back into her bed unless she meant more to him than a passing pleasure. With a child on the way, the stakes were too high to give him that kind of power over her since she wasn't the kind of woman who could simply indulge herself for the sake of…indulging.

Starting tomorrow, there wouldn't be any more impromptu meetings in private spaces where they could be totally alone. She needed allies. Distractions.

She needed family.

With that kind of buffer to romance, Delia would carefully insulate herself from temptation until Jager saw reason. Until he understood how much it hurt her to think about marrying for purely legal reasons. She'd already been a means to an end for one man. Now? She would never marry for anything less than love.

Jager stared at his cell phone as his call went through to the Manhattan number.

He didn't want to speak to any of his half brothers and hated relying on anyone else to find Damon. But tonight's discovery that Delia was pregnant left him with limited options. He needed to be with her to press his suit for marriage and, even more important, to make sure she remained in good health throughout her pregnancy. The realization that her mother had died in childbirth had left him reeling far more than the news that he was going to be a father.

He wouldn't let anything happen to Delia, or to their child. And if that meant making a deal with his father's other sons in New York, Jager would do it. He couldn't search for his missing brother and win over Delia too.

"Cameron McNeill," his half brother answered. It was a name Jager might never get used to hearing.

Until two months ago, Damon, Gabe and he were the only ones in his life who shared the same last name and the same useless father.

"It's Jager," he announced, pacing around his upstairs bedroom balcony. He could see a corner of the carriage house below. Delia's lights were all out now.

"Hello, brother." The greeting wasn't exactly sarcastic. But not entirely friendly either.

Hell. Maybe it was simply awkward. Jager could totally empathize with that, at least.

"I've decided to call in the favor you offered last time you were here." He lowered himself to sit on the giant chaise longue—another new addition to the house's furnishings under Delia's supervision. Everything about the historic Martinique property was warmer and more comfortable since she'd taken over.

"The favor I offered the time you locked me out and refused to see me?"

"Correct."

While he waited for Cam to respond, Jager could hear the familiar music from a popular video game.

He'd read—during a brief, unwelcome need to acquaint himself with the other branch of the family—that Cameron had founded a video game development company.

"I'm glad you're willing to have this conversation," Cameron finally said as the triumphant music that signaled he'd completed another game level played in the background. "Gramps is going to be psyched."

Jager stared out over the cottage and the gardens beyond just as some of the landscape lights shut off for the night.

"I'm not going to New York anytime soon," he warned his half brother. His grandfather had been pushing for a visit, but he had too many things to focus on at home. "I want to see if your investigator has any more luck than I've had finding Damon."

"Fine." A series of electronic chimes sounded on the other end of the call. "But when Bentley finds your brother, you're getting on a plane and meeting Malcolm."

He'd been expecting this, of course, but didn't appreciate being dictated to.

"Or Malcolm can get on a plane and meet all of us at once." Jager made the counteroffer mostly because he didn't like caving on this point. But he knew Delia wanted him to make peace with his family.

"Not happening," Cam said flatly. "It's not his fault Liam is a tool."

That shocked a laugh out of Jager. Not enough to concede the point, however.

"We can revisit the subject after your investigator finds my brother. There's no use planning for an event that could be totally hypothetical anyhow. And I'm not going to see any of you unless I've got Damon back." It would take something major to get him to change his mind. He fisted his hand against the lounger cushion, then pounded it twice.

"Very well. I'm texting you Bentley's contact information. He has reason to believe Damon's in Baja." Even as Cameron said the words, Jager heard the message notification chime in his ear.

The words confirmed what Jager had already feared. Damon had circled back to North America without telling anyone.

"He's trying to find the men he believes kidnapped his wife." A cold pit widened in his stomach.

Though he and Damon hadn't always seen eye to eye, Damon remained his younger brother. And, to an extent, his responsibility. He'd understood that even before their mother died of breast cancer when Jager was a senior in high school. With no father in the picture, it had always been Jager's job to make sure his siblings were safe.

"Or else he believes Caroline is still alive," Cameron offered, "and he wants to find her."

The words chilled him. Mostly because he feared that wasn't possible. He'd seen for himself how in love Caroline had been with his brother. He couldn't imagine her leaving of her own free will.

"For Damon's sake, I hope the latter is true." He needed some shred of positive news. "I'm going to phone Bentley now."

"Jager?" Cam said in a rush. "One more thing?"

He waited.

"You remember the terms of Malcolm's will? That we can only claim a share of his legacy if we've been married for twelve months?"

Jager's gaze shifted back to the cottage where Delia must be sleeping by now. He felt a pang of guilt that she'd taken the pregnancy test alone, that he hadn't been with her. What would she think about his wedding proposal if she discovered that marriage fulfilled one of the stipulations Malcolm McNeill had outlined for his heirs? Would she be so enthusiastic about a McNeill family union then, if she discovered another "business reason" for marriage?

"We don't want your company." He was more interested in profiting from his own projects—work he'd invested in personally.

"Right." Cameron huffed out a long sigh. "Between me and you, I'm grateful about that, so thanks. But our grandfather is a stubborn individual and he is determined to make us all fall in line."

"You're welcome to be his puppet. But not me." He was already grappling with feeling a lack of control where Delia was concerned. He wasn't about to relinquish more power over his own life to Malcolm McNeill.

"So consider a cash settlement," Cam suggested. "Meet Malcolm, shake his hand, let him feel like you're going to be a part of the family. But if you don't want the company, let my brothers and me buy you out."

"You can't be serious." The net worth of McNeill Resorts was staggering to contemplate. Far more than they'd make on the sale of Transparent, Damon's software company.

"Dead serious. Don't rob us of the business that has his name on it. The business we've all worked our asses off to further because it means something to him."

That Cameron would even suggest such an offer brought home how much he wanted to keep his grandfather's company intact. Interesting, because all three of the New York McNeill brothers were wealthy in their own right, with diverse business interests. Quinn, the oldest, was a hedge fund manager. He was *made* of money. So good with it, he earned millions showing other people what to invest in.

"I'll talk to my brothers," Jager finally conceded, levering himself off the chaise, needing to make his next call. "No promises though."

"That's all I'm asking."

Disconnecting the call, Jager checked his texts and found the contact information for the investigator Cameron had mentioned. As much as he hated asking for help to find Damon, Jager couldn't deny that he'd benefit from assistance after spending six weeks to find out something that this investigator had apparently known about for over a month. If he'd just given in and taken Cam up on the offer for help back when he showed up at the gate that night, maybe Jager would already have Damon back home.

It seemed stubbornness ran in the family, if what Cameron said about their grandfather was true.

For the first time since learning about his half-siblings, Jager thought maybe it wouldn't be so bad to at least meet them. Especially now that he was having a child of his own. Jager's father might be a two-timing failure as a role model, but that didn't necessarily mean Malcolm would be a negative influence on his heirs.

In less than nine months, Jager would need to make the decision. But first, his main concern was protecting Delia.

A job which would be easier as soon as she was his wife.

Six

With the top down on Jager's sporty convertible roadster, the warm December sun shining on them as they headed south the next day, Delia could almost forget they were driving toward her hometown.

She slicked on lip balm from her purse to keep from fidgeting as she was hit with a small attack of nerves. She'd avoided her father's fishing village for almost two years, preferring to coax him into Le François to visit her so she didn't need to run into people from her hometown. So many of her former neighbors had been at her failed wedding, witnessing the most humiliating day of her life. Understandably, going back home made her nervous. But she took comfort from the scent of the rich leather bucket seats and the smooth purr of the new Mercedes's engine. A local dealer had been all too glad to deliver a vehicle to Jager this morning, encouraging him to take the polar-white luxury car for a "test spin" for a week or two.

The privileged life her former boss led was going to be the kind of life that belonged to her child as well. But not to her. Delia had been lured in by the comforts of excess once. She wouldn't be wooed with superficial things again.

She chucked the lip balm back into her handbag as the vehicle slowed.

"That smells amazing," Jager observed as they stopped at a four-way intersection. "What is it?"

He peered over at her from the driver's seat, his blue gaze moving to her newly-shiny lips. It took all her willpower not to lick them. She felt incredibly aware of him today and she wasn't sure if it had to do with pregnancy hormones or the fact that she hadn't spent much time with him since their single combustible encounter in his office. She knew him differently now, and she wasn't sure she'd ever be able to look at him again without heat creeping all over her skin.

She straightened in her seat, hoping none of what she was thinking showed on her face.

"It's a new addition to the McNeill Meadows gift shop." She hadn't mentioned the product line to him, hoping to see the homemade beauty and bath items start turning a solid profit first. "I've been using the flower petals from the gardens, and beeswax from our beekeeper to make locally sourced lip balms and sugar scrubs. This one is called Coming Up Roses."

His gaze lingered on her mouth. Her heart skipped a beat or twelve.

"May I see?" he asked. With no one else at the intersection, he didn't seem in any hurry to put the car back in gear.

She did lick her lips then. "Um. There's no color or anything. It's just a balm." Still, she tilted toward him slightly so he could have a better look. The consistency of the product was really nice and she was proud of it.

"I meant the packaging." A grin twitched behind those words. "Although it looks very appealing on you."

"Oh." She leaned down to dig through her purse, wishing he didn't make her feel so fluttery inside. How was she going to forge a balanced, even relationship with him when she felt like a swooning teen around this man? "Here you go."

Passing him the tin, she tried to focus, bracing herself for the questions he might ask. But he seemed distracted today. Worried, perhaps. She wasn't sure if it was about the baby news or about his brother, but she understood he was coping with a lot right now. Businesswise, he was brokering a deal for the sale of Transparent, and that alone had to be stressful when it involved so much money.

"This was a great idea," he said finally, handing

her back the tin before another car arrived across from them at the intersection. Jager took his foot off the brake and they continued their trip. "I like the way you kept the farm-to-table sensibility with local ingredients."

"And," she couldn't resist adding, "I'm creating a mini exhibit in the gift area about the plantation history of the McNeill home. I think visitors will be interested that we're using our own sugarcane in the lip and body scrubs."

"We are?"

"I sent you some paperwork on it last spring," she reminded him, beginning to see familiar sights out the window as her village neared. "We made an arrangement with a small refinery in Florida, but the end product is very much locally sourced."

The private marina where her wedding would have been held was ahead on the right. She hadn't seen it since that day she'd stolen a Jet Ski that—thankfully—Jager had returned to the owner on her behalf. It had taken her a full year to repay him for the damages to the watercraft. Her nerves knotted tighter.

"Delia?" Jager said a moment later, making her wonder if she'd missed something he'd said.

"Hmm?" She pulled her gaze off the rocky coastline and back to the too-appealing father of her child.

She had to keep reminding herself of the fact since it still didn't feel real that she was carrying a McNeill heir.

"Are you nervous about seeing your father? Returning home?"

"Is it that obvious?" Her voice was a fraction of its usual volume. She cleared her throat. "I suppose it must be. And I'm not sure what has me more keyed up—telling my father I'm expecting, or seeing that marina where I stole a Jet Ski to escape from my ex."

"Would you like me to take a detour?" Jager flicked on the directional. "We can head inland for the last mile or two."

"No." She reached for him, laying a hand on his arm to stop him. "That's definitely not necessary. It's bad enough I was too insecure to handle things differently two years ago. I won't resort to running away anymore."

Resolutely, she looked out the driver's-side window, where the first boats of the marina were coming into view, bobbing in the crystalline blue water. The scent of the sea drifted through the convertible. Her hand fell away from his strong forearm.

If she touched him too long, she might not be able to stop.

"You didn't run away," he replied, his jaw flexing as he flicked his gaze out the side window for a moment before returning his attention to the road. "You escaped a bad situation. Big difference."

"There's no good excuse for larceny." The guilt over doing something so foolish still gnawed at her on occasion, but her actions that day hadn't just been in response to her fiancé's deception. "Although I might have been able to face my wedding guests that day if I hadn't also learned that my father knew about Brandon's involvement with the investment company."

They cruised past the permanent archway installed on the pier where people traveled from all over the world to say their vows. Today, in fact, a Christmas bride carrying a bouquet of red roses stood beside her tuxedoed groom, a blanket of poinsettias draping the arch. A small crowd filled the pier to watch, just the way Delia's guests had gathered two years ago.

"Your father knew?" Jager asked, his tone incredulous. He didn't even seem to notice the wedding in progress. "Didn't he care that jackass fiancé of yours was going to try to steal away your inheritance?"

That's exactly how she'd felt at the time, but her father had been unperturbed when she approached him in tears.

"Dad said the land was always meant for me, so if I wanted to sell it to developers, that was my business." It had been the way he'd said it that had hurt the most, with a shrug as if it didn't matter to him either way.

It had confirmed for Delia what she'd feared since childhood—that her father watched over her out of a sense of duty, never a sense of love. Pascal Rickard was a hard man, and she'd told herself for years he was simply too stoic to show his softer emotions. On her disastrous wedding day, she'd been confronted with evidence that he really didn't care all that much, and it had been a hurt deeper than anything Brandon Nelson could have ever doled out.

"You never told me." Jager gripped the stick shift tightly as he slowed down the vehicle. "All this time I thought it was a broken heart that brought you to my island that day."

He'd been like a mirage in the desert that day, a too-good-to-be-true vision of masculinity and caring as he helped her out from under the broken Jet Ski. She'd thrown herself into his open arms like he was an old friend and not a total stranger. Funny how she'd worked for two years to erase the horrible first impression she'd made, only to fall right back into those strong arms at his slightest invitation.

"It was a broken heart." She breathed in the scent of spices and fish as they neared the village market near the water. "But Brandon only accounted for part of it."

When Jager didn't respond, she tried to gauge his expression. He turned down the side road that led to her father's property, a tiny white-and-blue fish shack on the corner open for business. A few tourists lined up for whatever they were frying up today, the picnic tables out front already filled.

Tourist season started in December, and even the small fishing villages like this one benefited from the extra traffic.

"No wonder you haven't wanted to return here," Jager muttered darkly. "He would have let you walk right into marriage with a guy who wanted to steal your birthright."

True. But over time, Delia had come to see her father's point of view. He'd assumed that Delia was forsaking the land for the comforts of marriage to a local businessman with more financial means than she'd had growing up. And, sometimes, she feared that he'd understood her more than she understood herself, since walking away from Brandon hadn't been nearly as difficult as it should have been. How much had she loved her former fiancé in the first place?

Clearly, her judgment in men could not be trusted.

"Do you remember which one it is?" She pointed to the bright red house on stilts. "It's over there."

Nodding, Jager pulled off the main street onto the pitted driveway that led to her father's cabin, the simple home where she'd been raised. All around them, she knew, were other families who'd wanted desperately to sell their properties to the development group that had planned to put in an airstrip for a luxury resort. Her father had been the lone holdout.

For as long as he could pay the taxes. Because even though that old deal was no longer on the table, the plans were a matter of public record. Any other developer could swoop in and re-create the plan if they were able to obtain the necessary parcels of land to make it happen.

Tension seized up her shoulders as Jager stopped the car and came around to open her door. It was easier to simply send checks home than to face her father again after all this time. But today, for her child's sake, she needed answers that only Pascal Rickard could provide.

So for just a moment, she took comfort from Jager's hand around hers as he helped her from the Mercedes. She lingered for a moment as they stood close together, her sundress blowing lightly against his legs and winding around him the way the rest of her wanted to. She breathed in the scent of his aftershave—woodsy and familiar—before forcing herself to step away.

She'd allowed too many men access to her heart, and the price for her lack of judgment had been high—broken relationships and too much hurt. She wouldn't make the same mistake with Jager. As the father of her child, he was someone she needed to remain friends with. Only friends.

Forever.

Jager could practically see the mental suit of armor Delia put on as they entered her father's house. Hell, he'd done the same thing long ago himself, back when his family had still been living in the United States and he'd been young enough to care what his father thought of him.

Delia's careful mask of indifference reminded him of things from his own past he didn't want to recall.

So while she made awkward small talk with the serious, graying fisherman, Jager focused on his own agenda for the day. He needed to find out as many details as possible about the cause of her mother's death. Once he had ferreted out all the information, he would consult physicians independently.

Because while Delia had made a doctor's appointment for that afternoon, he didn't trust the local obstetrician to be on the forefront of prenatal and preventative healthcare. The one benefit he could see of a trip to New York—and to the home of the McNeill patriarch—was to ensure Delia had the best possible doctors for this baby.

Their baby.

The idea still threatened to level him every time he thought about it.

Now he followed Delia and her father outside to the deck overlooking the water. The red cabin on stilts was one of many brightly painted houses the village website touted as "charming," but Jager knew Delia's upbringing had been rough. She'd worked hard to help her father make a living, checking nets and making repairs almost daily, manning the fish market when he needed to go back out to sea and cleaning fish for demanding customers.

Still, there was beauty here in the simplicity of a lifestyle rooted in a sense of community. Jager envied that, especially after the McNeill wealth had attracted the kidnappers who'd taken Damon's wife.

Jager would never forget the naked pain in his brother's eyes the day she'd gone missing. The day she'd been presumed dead by the police.

Taking a seat beside Delia, Jager ached to touch her. Hold her hand and tell her father in no uncertain terms that he would be taking take care of Delia from now on. But until she agreed to marriage, what right did he have to stake that claim?

Clamping his jaw shut tight, he studied the older man. Even in his seventies, Pascal Rickard possessed a much younger man's vitality. His half arm didn't seem to hinder him much, and he used the partial limb efficiently enough, easily swinging an extra chair into place at the rickety patio table so that they could all have a seat. When her father didn't offer them anything, Delia returned inside, emerging a minute later with a pitcher of ice water and clear blue glasses. Jager stood to help her pour, passing around the drinks, and then they both sat again.

Had she always taken care of her father that way? Jager wondered. The older man sipped his water without comment while Delia spoke.

"Daddy, I'm here today because I need to ask you a few questions about my mother. About how she died." Leaning forward in her rusted metal seat, Delia clutched her water glass in both hands, the tension in her arms belying the calm tone of her voice. "I know you don't like to talk about her. But it's important to me now because I'm pregnant."

Jager hadn't expected her to launch right into the heart of the matter. He guessed it must have been nerves that propelled the words from her, because she wasn't the kind of woman to shock an old man on purpose.

Pascal's face paled for a moment while he sipped his drink. Then he lowered the glass to the lopsided wooden tabletop.

"That's why you're here?" Pascal asked Jager, his hazel eyes the same shade as his daughter's but without any of the tenderness.

"I have asked Delia to marry me," Jager pointed out, reaching for her hand on instinct. "I hope that I will convince her to accept before our child is born."

Long before then, actually. Tomorrow wasn't soon enough as far as he was concerned.

Pascal grunted. Some of the color returned to his face, but his expression remained stony. Delia, at least, allowed Jager to hold her hand.

"I'm seeing an obstetrician later today," Delia continued as if Jager hadn't spoken. "And I need more details about mom's medical history in case there could be genetic factors at work we should know about."

The idea punched through Jager again as he turned to watch her. He'd lost his own mother too early, and Delia had never known hers. He guessed the vision of a child growing up without a mother was equally real for both of them. The thought had him twining his fingers through Delia's slender ones, gripping her tighter.

Pascal thrust his lower lip forward in an expression of disapproval before he turned to address Jager again. "Delia doesn't want to get married. Didn't she tell you? She could have been settled by now, but she didn't want to share her inheritance with developers."

Defensiveness rose in him, all the more when he heard Delia's soft gasp of surprise.

"Her fiancé had no plans of 'sharing' it," Jager reminded him. "Something he failed to mention to your daughter. She had to discover on her own." He pressed on, remembering how hurt Delia had been the day she'd wrecked that Jet Ski on the beach. "Didn't it occur to you she'd want to know Brandon's reason for marrying her?"

The old man shrugged, settling his empty water glass on the peeling, planked floor. "She seemed happy enough to put this life behind her when she was dating her big spender."

"That's not fair." Delia shot out of her chair, stalking to the half wall surrounding the deck. "I thought Brandon cared about me."

"And I thought you cared about making a better life for yourself," her father retorted, tipping back in the wooden dining chair he'd dragged outside from the kitchen. "Brandon offered you more than a life as his mistress."

Anger flared hot. Jager deliberately remained seated, facing her father head-on before he replied, "I am prepared to give Delia my home, my name and my life. I thought I made that clear. Right now, I would appreciate your help in protecting her health, so I'd like to know if this pregnancy poses a serious risk for her."

"And if it does?" Pascal set the feet of his chair back on the floor with a thud. "What then? Are you still prepared to give my daughter your life and your name if she can't carry your child to term? Or are you only willing to marry her for a McNeill heir?"

"Daddy, please." Delia stepped closer, not quite between them, but definitely in an effort to placate her father. She touched his knee and dropped down to sit on an overturned milk crate beside him. "I will decide my future, but I need to know what I'm facing. If you don't know about my mother's medical history, maybe you could tell me the name of her doctor—"

Pascal cut her off with a quick shake of his head. "Celine didn't have anything genetic." The words sounded raw in his throat, far different from the taunting tone he'd taken with Jager a minute ago. "She never even told me until that night on the boat when you were born, but Celine had a cesarean as a young woman when she gave birth to a stillborn child. She'd been frightened of something going wrong again. Worried she'd disappoint me." He swallowed hard and looked out to sea, unable to continue for a moment. "By the time I knew about it, it was too late. We'd only been married for two years."

The anger Jager had been feeling toward him seeped away then, his own fears for Delia making it too easy to identify with him.

"Afterward," her father continued, "when I got back to shore with you, the doctors said a cesarean can cause a uterine rupture later in life. It's rare, but it happens. Your mother had no idea of the risk, I'm certain of that, because she wanted you. Desperately."

Jager waited for Delia to ask him more, but she'd gone quiet. She studied her father, who remained silent.

Leaving Jager no choice but to step in again.

"Why was Celine's first child stillborn?" he asked, wanting to give Delia's doctor a complete picture of any relevant medical history.

Delia spun away from them on the milk crate, grabbing her bag and riffling through the purse before coming up with a tissue.

Had he said something wrong?

Pascal shook his head. "I couldn't tell you. Celine never told me anything about that time in her life until the night she died."

Damn it. Jager kept digging. "Was she from this village? Maybe we can speak to her doctor."

Pascal folded his good arm over the injured limb, his mouth set in a thin line. Delia seemed to read this as a rejection of the question or refusal to reply, because she stepped closer again, slipping her hand around Jager's elbow.

"I can find out about those things," she assured him quietly. Her eyes were bright but there were no tears. "We should go."

Jager wanted to argue, to find out what else they could glean from her father. But seeing the hurt in Delia's eyes—a hurt he didn't fully understand—he followed her outside after a terse goodbye to Pascal. He didn't want to gainsay her in front of her father, a stunt that definitely wouldn't help his efforts to win her hand. He would simply call in every resource to learn more about Celine's medical condition. For now, they had enough information for Delia's obstetrician appointment.

It was good news that the uterine condition wasn't genetic. Yet there was still the worry of why her mother had a stillborn child when she'd been a younger woman. Jager's gut knotted as he opened the passenger door of the convertible for Delia.

No doubt she was upset about that news too, because she retreated to her side of the vehicle and didn't have a single word to say on the ride to her doctor's appointment.

Seven

Stepping out of the exam room an hour later, Delia smoothed a hand through her hair, still windswept from the car ride with the top down. While she was in the cold, antiseptic-scented room with the nurse and her new doctor, Delia had been very aware of Jager's presence in the waiting area outside. The nurse had said she would bring him back to the doctor's private office so they could both speak with the obstetrician at the same time.

After their meeting with her father, Delia had had a fair idea of how that encounter would go. Jager would ask the questions and push for answers.

With the doctor, she wouldn't mind so much. But with her father…

She paused a few steps from the doctor's office, closed her eyes and pulled in a deep breath. Remembering how close she'd been to hearing her father confess something—love for her? That she'd been loved by her mother?—pinched her emotions hard. Today had been the closest her father had ever come to showing some paternal warmth for her when he'd said that her mother had wanted her *desperately*.

How long had she yearned for scraps of his affection, even if that fondness was only a pale reflection of the love her mother might have given her? But the moment when he might have said more had evaporated forever when Jager interrupted, pushing the conversation in a more pragmatic direction.

He didn't know, of course, how much those few words from her father had meant. How much she craved even a few. So she couldn't blame him for stamping out any possibility that the stoic Pascal would share some tender memory from his past.

And yet, she did.

She'd wanted to see her father alone, but Jager had insisted on being a part of her pregnancy. She needed to start building boundaries with him fast before she lost her sense of self to the strong will of this McNeill male. The past two years had been full of hard work to prove to herself she was smart, independent and capable. Being pregnant couldn't take that away from her.

"Ms. Rickard?" The voice of the doctor, a young

woman fresh from her residency in Miami, startled Delia.

She opened her eyes and faced Dr. Ruiz. Tall and willowy, the physician wore a light-up reindeer pin on the lapel of her white lab coat over a red tartan dress.

"Yes." Straightening, Delia told herself to get it together. "Sorry. I'm just…excited. About the baby news." She babbled awkwardly, embarrassed to be caught doing relaxation breathing in the middle of the hallway. "It's a lot to process."

"Come on in the office," the doctor urged, opening the door to the consultation room. "I'll do what I can to help you both."

Dr. Ruiz introduced herself to Jager and they settled into chairs around the obstetrician's desk as she talked through the preliminaries. Yes, they'd confirmed her pregnancy. Delia was given a piece of paper with her summer due date written on it in black marker.

Her hand crept to her flat belly while she tried to take it all in. Once more, Jager took the lead with questions, sharing his concerns about her mother's health history and the stillbirth. But when he launched into more questions about the uterine rupture too, Delia interrupted.

"My father made it clear that wasn't a genetic condition," she reminded him before turning to Dr. Ruiz. A filing cabinet behind the obstetrician had a magnet that said Keep Calm and Get Your Pap On caught Delia's eye.

Jager reached over and rested a hand on the back of her chair, so that he was barely touching her. "But your father's not a physician. Perhaps Dr. Ruiz will view the information differently."

Delia felt the sting of defensiveness despite the inevitable rush of heat from Jager's touch. Did he think she was incapable of relating her own medical history? "My mother had a cesarean. I've never had one. I've never even been pregnant."

Dr. Ruiz gave a brisk nod and glanced down at her notes. "I think we'd all rest easier with some more information about your mother's medical history." Her red-polished fingernail trailed down over the chart. "She's from Martinique?"

"Yes. She moved to Le Vauclin after she married my father, but she was raised in Sainte-Anne." Delia knew so little about her mother or her mother's family. According to Pascal, Celine's parents had died in a car crash when she was in high school.

The doctor scribbled a note on a Post-it while her reindeer pin blinked on and off. "I may be able to requisition some more information."

Jager squeezed Delia's hand. "Thank you."

She should be relieved. They did need more information about her mother's health history. Perhaps fear for her baby was making Delia unreasonably prickly when it came to Jager taking command of the conversation with both the physician and her father.

He had every bit as much reason to be concerned about this baby's health as she did. Still, something about the way the events had unfolded today made her feel like an afterthought.

He would never cherish her the way he cherished his child, of course. It rattled her to think that; in some small corner of her heart, she nursed a hope that she could be more than just a surrogate for a McNeill baby in Jager's eyes.

He took her hand in his. A show of tenderness for the doctor's sake? Or did the paternal feeling he fostered for his child come through in the way he touched her?

His blue gaze found hers for a moment before flicking back to the physician. "We will be looking for the most advanced care for a possible high-risk pregnancy. Can you recommend the best doctors or hospitals for this?"

Frowning, Delia slid her hand out from under his. "High risk?" Her heart rate sped up. Since when did she need the most advanced care? "We don't have any reason to believe I'm high risk."

"Not yet," Jager conceded with a nod. "But until we know the rest of your mother's history, it would be wise to have a plan in place."

The doctor paused in her note taking. "We've handled many high-risk pregnancies here. However, the most respected maternal fetal medicine facilities will be in the States. If you'd like a list—"

"We don't need a list," Delia informed Jager.

At the same moment, he nodded. "Thank you."

After a few more tense minutes in the consultation room, they departed. Delia stalked out ahead of him, clutching her file of papers about pregnancy with the due date and a prescription for prenatal vitamins.

She'd left Jager to take the paper containing names of maternal fetal specialists he'd requested.

"Delia." His voice was close behind her as she hurried through the parking lot with its lampposts connected by green garland swags dotted with red berries. "Please wait."

Her toes pinched in her high-heeled sandals. She wanted to be home with her feet up, surrounded by the fairy-tale paintings on her living room walls, a cup of tea in her hand. How had her life spun so far out of control so fast? She slowed her pace.

When he reached her side, he turned her to face him, his gaze sweeping over her in a way that shouldn't have incited a physical reaction and damned well did anyhow. It was like that one fateful encounter with him had stripped away all her defenses where he was concerned. Now she felt naked every time they were together.

"You're angry with me," he observed while a French Christmas carol hummed through a speaker system connected to the lampposts.

The chorus of "Un Flambeau, Jeannette, Isabelle" celebrated the beauty of a newborn child while he lay sleeping in a cradle. Something about the image resonated deeply. The lyrics were so familiar Delia could visualize the villagers admiring the new baby. Soon she would have a child of her own. More than anything she wanted to be a good mother. To stand beside the cradle of her newborn and protect that fragile life with a fierceness no one had ever showed to defend her.

"I'm frustrated that you commandeered our important conversation today." She wondered what Christmas would be like this year.

"Commandeered?" His brows swooped down. "I participated. The same way you did."

"I realize you are used to taking the lead," she continued, feeling more sure of herself as she spoke. If she was going to be an equal partner in parenting, she needed to lay the groundwork for it now. "But we'll need to find a way to rework our relationship so that you're not still trying to be my boss."

"I'm trying to protect you," he clarified. "And our child. That's different."

"And you were so focused on your own agenda that mine fell by the wayside." She straightened the strap on her sundress and felt his gaze track the movement.

She didn't like this confusing intersection point between attraction and frustration.

"I thought we shared the same agenda." Jager covered her bare shoulder with one hand, his fingers stroking a gentle touch along the back of her arm. "To find out answers that could help us protect your health, and the health of our child."

Unwelcome heat stirred from just that simple touch. The classic Christmas carol gave way to a holiday love song.

"I've waited my whole life to have a meaningful conversation with my father about the night I was born." In the past, she'd always backed away from the talk that he didn't want to have. "There were more answers I wanted from him."

He'd been close to saying more about that night. She was sure of it.

"I'm sorry." Jager's simple reply stole away her anger. She might not be able to read him all the time, but she recognized the remorse in his voice now, the obvious sincerity in his eyes. "I didn't know."

Behind them, a young family emerged from the doctor's office. The husband held the door for his wife as she pushed a toddler in a stroller. The woman's pregnant belly filled the front of a floral maternity dress.

Delia touched her own stomach, still flat. But she could see that ultrasound image so strongly in her mind. Would her child ever have a sibling? If she didn't accept Jager's offer of marriage—and she would not accept a business proposal—how soon would he move on with someone else?

"Come on." Jager wrapped an arm around her waist and guided her toward the convertible. "Let me apologize by taking you out for dinner."

"That's not necessary," she assured him, ready to retreat from the world. And the temptation he posed. "Thank you. But I'm tired."

Discouraged.

She strode ahead toward his car, hearing his steady steps behind her even as he seemed to take the hint and respect her need for silence. She needed to be stronger and smarter tomorrow. To be a worthy advocate for her unborn baby and weigh her options moving forward. If she was indeed a high-risk pregnancy, what did that mean for her? For her father? Would she have to quit working? Would she and her father lose the family lands after all she'd done to try to protect it?

The plot of Rickard acreage felt like one small offering she had to bring to her baby that was all hers, separate from the McNeill wealth. Perhaps because she had nothing of her mother's, Delia felt the need to be able to give her child something tangible. Something beyond the love she would bear this baby.

Opening the passenger-side door of the bright white vehicle, Jager helped her inside, passing her the seat belt buckle while she tucked her dress around her legs for the breezy ride with the top down. After he closed her door and came around and settled into the driver's seat beside her, he paused before switching on the ignition.

"Can I ask you something, or are we still not talking?" Jager rattled the car key lightly against the gearshift.

"Not funny. But say what you need to." Delia pressed deeper into the leather seat, tipping her neck back into the molded headrest.

"What else were you hoping to learn from Pascal?" He lowered his voice even though there was no one else parked nearby. The family they'd seen earlier was packing into a minivan on the other side of the lot.

She figured she might as well tell Jager the truth since they would be sharing parenting one day and this was very relevant. "It might sound juvenile, but my father has never once said he loved me." She forced a shrug so the words didn't come across as pathetic as they sounded. "I thought today might be the day."

In the moment of silence that followed, she appreciated Jager's restraint. If his response had hinted at any form of pity, she wasn't sure how she could have handled it on such an emotional afternoon.

"Our fathers are very different from one another," he observed finally. "Yours is stoic and undemonstrative even though he was with you throughout your childhood. Mine was fun and fully engaged when he was around, but for the vast majority of time, he was absent." His hand slid over her forearm where it rested on the leather console between them. "I guarantee you I'm not going to be like that with our child. I will be a presence. And I'll do whatever it takes to be a welcome one."

For a moment, she allowed herself to be comforted by the words. This man had been a good friend, after all, before she'd given in to her attraction to him. She could still admire his desire to be a better person.

"We have nine months to figure out a way to be good parents." She had no role model for motherhood, but if she could figure out how to manage and grow McNeill Meadows, which included the historic McNeill mansion and a successful farm-to-table community garden, she would learn about parenting too.

"Less than eight, according to your due date." Jager's hand slid away from her forearm as he moved to start the car. "Since we have a limited amount of time and a lot to accomplish, I'm going to suggest we schedule a trip to New York as soon as possible."

"New York?" The warmth she'd been feeling for him chilled. "Didn't we go over this in the doctor's office? I'm not going to see a specialist or be stressed about a possible high-risk pregnancy until we have some concrete reason to be concerned."

"I completely understand." He backed the car out of the spot. "But you've been adamant that I meet the rest of the McNeills and establish ties with my half brothers." He shot her a sideways glance as he shifted into first, his hand grazing her knee through the thin cotton of her dress. "My relations are going to be our child's relatives too. It makes sense that you visit New York with me and get acquainted with the extended McNeill family."

His words stunned her silent.

Six weeks ago, she had lobbied hard for him to meet his grandfather, Malcolm McNeill. That didn't mean she wanted to be introduced to one of the wealthiest men in the world as Jager's baby mama.

Holding up a trembling hand, she searched for an excuse, any excuse. "I have a lot of arrangements to make here. Things to do to get ready for the baby. And I can't afford to quit my job—"

"Delia." He shook his head. "As the mother of a McNeill, you can afford to do as you please. We'll close up the house in Martinique and spend some time in Manhattan getting to know the rest of the McNeills. If you thought it was a good idea for me to foster those relationships, you must think it's a good idea for our child."

How neatly he'd turned that argument around to maneuver her now. She couldn't think of an appropriate retort as Jager turned the vehicle back onto the westbound road toward Le François. As much as she wanted to retreat into her fairy-tale-painted cottage with her books and dreams, she knew her life would never be the same again. She needed to think like a mother.

Jager slipped his hand over hers, threading their fingers together now that he'd reached a cruising speed and didn't need to shift for a while.

He continued to speak, undeterred by her surprised silence. "If it turns out you need the added care of a specialized facility, we'll already be in New York. If not, you can dictate where you want to be when it comes time to give birth." He gave her hand a gentle squeeze. "You don't want to be traveling anywhere near the due date."

His words sent a chill through her. Her mother had been out on a boat the night she'd delivered prematurely and had paid the ultimate price. Delia felt sure that she wasn't going to be a high-risk pregnancy. But if she was thinking like a mother—putting her child first—she conceded that Jager had a point.

Accepting his help was in the best interest of their child.

She took a deep breath and let the wind whip through her hair as she tipped her head up to the blue sky. "When do we leave?"

Eight

Stepping off his grandfather's private jet onto the snowy tarmac of Teterboro Airport outside New York City eight days later, Jager wondered if he'd made a deal with the devil to coax Delia out of Martinique.

Jager hadn't wanted any of the McNeill red carpet treatment, and would have damned well preferred making his own travel arrangements, but wily old Malcolm had pulled strings to ensure the trip was exceptionally easy. With his connections, Malcolm had found a way to fast-track Delia as a trusted traveler, a designation Jager already had for himself. That streamlined their arrival process so efficiently that they didn't even need to clear customs in the airport.

The minute they got off the plane and went into the terminal, the limo driver was already visible with his white sign bearing the family name.

Jager hadn't been able to refuse his grandfather's help when it made things easier for Delia. No matter what her doctor said about her pregnancy being normal, he would continue to worry about her health and the health of their baby until they found out more about her mother's medical history. So far, Dr. Ruiz hadn't had any more luck unearthing facts about Celine's first pregnancy than Jager had, but the Martinique physician anticipated speaking to one of Celine's former doctors this week.

"What about our luggage?" Delia asked, shivering slightly as she peered back over her shoulder to stare up at the sleek Cessna, where the two crew members lingered.

Jager tugged her red plaid scarf up higher. He'd bought her warm clothes for the trip, including the long blue wool coat she wore belted tight. At seven weeks pregnant, she looked thinner to him, even in the coat. She insisted she hadn't experienced any morning sickness, but he'd checked it out online to make sure that was normal.

"The driver will make sure they're loaded in the car," Jager assured her, grateful for the cold so he had an excuse to wrap an arm around her and pull her to his side.

The past few days had been busy with preparations to spend Christmas in New York, and he'd tried to give her room to breathe. But he missed her now even more than he had after they'd spent those six weeks apart when he'd been searching Europe for Damon. Seeing her every day, knowing she was carrying his child, only made him want her more. He hoped spending the holidays together would bring them closer.

"Do you always travel like this?" She ducked her head toward his chest, her silky blond hair brushing the lapel of his gray overcoat that hadn't been out of his closet in two years.

"Definitely not." He'd traveled around the world on his own dime—an experience he'd been fortunate to afford—but never with an army of personal staff members. "The added luxury is courtesy of my grandfather."

Did Malcolm think he could bribe him to come into the family fold? Pay him off to accept his father back into his life?

Not happening.

"I know you're only having this meeting with him for our child's sake." She matched her pace to his while the driver hurried over to greet them and send two skycaps out to take their bags.

"And for yours." Jager couldn't help but point that out since he was doing everything in his power to convince Delia he would make a good partner. A good husband. "I wouldn't be in New York right now if it wasn't for you." It was something Delia had really encouraged since she wanted their child to have a bigger family than she'd known growing up.

They walked quickly through the terminal. Christmas trees decorated the crowded lobby, filling the soaring space with the scent of pine. With just a few days left until Christmas, Jager needed to move up his timetable to convince Delia to marry him. Ideally, he'd have a Christmas Eve proposal—one that she'd accept—and a New Year's wedding. Once that was settled, he'd be able to turn his attention back to the sale of Transparent and finding Damon, both of which needed to happen before he could have any kind of meaningful conversation with Malcolm McNeill about their position within the family. Jager couldn't make those decisions without Damon's input. But for now, he could at least meet his grandfather.

"I hope one day you'll be glad you made this concession to come here." Her cheeks were flushed from the cold as they stepped back outside again toward the waiting Mercedes sedan.

The driver, Paolo, directed the loading of their bags while Jager helped Delia into the passenger area in back. Her high-heeled black boots were visible beneath the hem of her coat, the soft suede molded to slim calves. For nearly two weeks, he'd been attuned to small details like that, from the way she tipped her head back when she laughed, to the delicate habit she had of brushing her fingers over her flat belly when she thought no one noticed. As if reassuring herself there was life inside her.

He looked forward to the day she was cleared for intimacy by her doctor, and to the day she trusted him enough to welcome him back into her bed, so he too could lay his palm on the soft expanse of skin between her hips.

Once she was safely inside the vehicle, Jager took Paolo aside.

"We're staying at The Plaza," he informed him. "That's our first stop."

The tall, athletically built driver looked like he could serve double duty as private security on the side with his dark coat and sunglasses. "But Mr. McNeill said to bring you directly to the house."

"Miss Rickard has had a long journey." Jager moved closer to the vehicle. "I'll call my grandfather to explain personally."

The driver's bronzed forehead furrowed, but he nodded. "As you wish."

They had been invited to stay at the McNeill home, a private fourteen-thousand-square-foot townhouse on the Upper East Side. It was a historic piece of local architecture that Jager would normally look forward to seeing, but he had no intention of taking up residence under the family roof. He had tried explaining that to Cameron without much luck. Jager had yet to converse with Malcolm directly.

Inside the limousine, he realized Delia was listening intently to her cell phone.

"Dr. Ruiz?" she said into the mouthpiece as her eyes lifted to meet Jager's gaze. "I'm going to put you on speakerphone. Could you repeat that last part for Jager's sake?"

The obstetrician must have news. About Delia's health? Or about the mystery of Celine's medical history?

"Yes. Hello." The lightly accented voice of the doctor came through the phone. The sound quality was tinny and diminished, but Jager was so glad to hear from her. "Mr. McNeill, I was just explaining to Delia that her mother suffered from lupus. She didn't see a doctor regularly for the condition, and was unaware of the disease with her first pregnancy."

Jager sat knee to knee with Delia in the wide leather seat. At some point, he'd taken her hand, and he squeezed it now. A smile kicked up one side of her mouth, reminding him that it had been too long since he'd seen her happy. They'd both been so worried about this.

"What about Delia? Could she have the condition and be unaware?" His heart lodged in his throat.

"No." Dr. Ruiz sounded certain. "We did a complete blood workup when she was here and I had enough to run additional tests once we received the news about her mother. The test for lupus is one of the most sensitive diagnostic indicators for the disease, clearing Delia with 98% certainty. And since she has virtually no other symptoms—"

Relief coursed through him with a *whoosh* in his

ears that drowned out whatever else the obstetrician had to say. He'd been concerned for Delia's health, and for their child's, but he hadn't fully understood how truly scared he was until that moment. His chest constricted. He wrapped his arms around Delia and held her tight. To hell with giving her space.

Inhaling the warm vanilla fragrance of her hair, he smoothed his cheek along the silky strands. Even through the layers of their coats, he could feel the gentle swell of her curves. He traced circles on her back with one hand, soothing himself even as he offered her comfort. Connection.

"Mr. McNeill?" Dr. Ruiz's tinny voice echoed in the limo. "If you have any other questions for me—"

"Just one," he answered, turning his head to be better heard since he wasn't ready to release Delia yet. "I want to be sure I understand. You're saying that Delia is healthy enough for all normal activity?"

Delia turned her face up and peered into his eyes. Her gaze was quizzical for only a moment. And then she must have read his mind, because her cheeks colored with a heat he remembered well. It occurred to him how much he enjoyed her pale complexion that betrayed her so easily.

"Absolutely." Dr. Ruiz's smile was evident in the tone of her voice. "Congratulations to you both. You have all the signs of a healthy pregnancy."

Delia's forehead tipped onto his shoulder, but she didn't move away from him as Jager thanked the doctor for the good news and disconnected the call.

As the Mercedes sped south on I-95, Jager stroked Delia's hair, the strands clinging from static. When she lifted her face to look at him, her hazel eyes were greener than usual—bright with a mix of emotions he couldn't read.

"Looks like Manhattan is good luck for us." He couldn't help the heated edge in his voice as he unfastened the belt on her bright blue coat and slid a hand over her waist.

Her long gray sweater dress skimmed her subtle curves. If they weren't riding in a car, he would have slid a hand under her knees and tugged her onto his lap.

"Because I'm healthy enough to carry a baby to term, or because I just had the green light for intimacy?" She arched an eyebrow at him, but the rapid tattoo of her pulse at her neck gave away how much the idea intrigued her too.

"My concern is for you and our baby. You know that." He had battled bad dreams for the last week and a half. Every time Delia was in a boat out to sea where he couldn't reach her. Each time, he'd awoken sweating and tangled in his sheets. "But I won't deny that I've thought about being with you again."

She tensed beneath his touch as the limo jockeyed for position on the way into the Lincoln Tunnel. The last rays of afternoon sun disappeared when they descended. Shadows played over her face between flashes of the tunnel's fluorescent lighting.

"I've thought about being with you too." She

didn't sound happy about it, and he noticed how she was nervously twisting a button on his coat cuff with her fingers. "But I can't afford to lose perspective where you're concerned. Not when our relationship is already so convoluted and I can't trust my judgment with men."

He hated that her ex had made her doubt herself so much. Jager willed himself to find the right words that would make her see his point of view.

"Delia." He took both of her hands in both of his. "You've known me for two years. I gave you a job because I admired the way you didn't let the pressure of society sway you into marrying Brandon. I thought escaping your wedding on a Jet Ski was kick-ass."

She shook her head. "I was scared."

"But you didn't let fear stop you. You set a course and got the hell out of Dodge."

A tiny ghost of a smile appeared on her face. "You're being generous."

"I'm being honest. I liked you right away, and I believe that feeling was mutual from the very first day." He tipped her chin up when she looked away, needing to see her eyes to track her reaction to his words. "You know my brothers. You know my business dealings. Have I ever given you reason to think I've tried to hide something from you the way Brandon did?"

"Never." She said the word softly but with a fierceness that made his heart turn over.

"Then trust me when I say that you are the most

important part of my life right now." He brought one of her hands to his lips and kissed it, then the other. "The last thing I want to do is hurt you, and I can promise if anything makes you unhappy, I'm going to do everything in my power to fix it."

His heart beat harder, as if he could somehow hammer home the words with the force of his will. He could see the struggle in her eyes. The worry that another man had put there. Hell, even her father had made her doubt herself, so he couldn't blame Brandon for that.

Slowly, however, her smile reappeared as the limo hit Midtown. A sexy glimmer lit her hazel eyes as if she'd just started thinking something…naughty.

"I'm going to hold you to that promise, Jager McNeill."

"I hope you do." Desire for her thrummed in his veins, a slow, simmering heat that had him hauling open the door of the vehicle as soon as it pulled up to the curb in front of The Plaza Hotel.

Helping her from the car onto the red carpet underneath the flags that waved over the iconic entrance to the hotel across from Central Park, he was more than ready to bring her to their room. To kiss every inch of her.

And remind her how good they could be together.

But he'd forgotten she'd never been to New York. Let alone Central Park. Or The Plaza Hotel.

At Christmastime.

Her eyes glowed as she stepped out of the limo,

and the pleasure he saw there didn't have anything to do with him.

"It's so beautiful!" she exclaimed, doing a slow twirl to take it all in, just like every starry-eyed tourist to ever clog up a city street at rush hour.

Despite his thwarted libido, he couldn't resist the chance to make Delia Rickard happy.

"Would you like a tour?" he asked her, waving off Paolo and the hotel doormen, who were ready to assist with their every need.

"Yes!" She was already gazing at a horse-drawn carriage across the street, her body swaying slightly to the strains of a Christmas tune emanating from a trio of musicians near the park entrance.

Jager forced his gaze away from her and told himself to get a grip. This was the chance he'd been waiting for, and he wasn't about to waste it.

"Don't let go." Delia wrapped a hand around Jager's waist and her other around his neck. "Please. Whatever you do? Don't let go."

Teetering on thin blades, she let Jager tug her around the slippery ice skating rink while other holiday revelers whizzed past them. Even knee-high children skated quickly past, their blades making a *skritch, skritch* sound in the cold ice, cutting tiny swaths and sometimes lifting a fine, snow-like spray in their wake.

Her first time on ice skates was a little scarier than she'd anticipated. After a tour of the Christmas lights around Central Park and down Fifth Avenue, she and Jager had stopped at a food cart for gyros. She'd been entranced by the sight of the huge Christmas tree in Rockefeller Plaza. Even better? The ice-skaters skimming the expanse of bright white below the noble fir. She hadn't hesitated when Jager asked if she wanted to test her skills on skates.

Clearly, she'd been too caught up in the holiday spirit to think about what she was getting into. Now Dean Martin crooned about letting it snow on the speaker system, but even with all the laughter, happy shouts and twinkling lights around her, Delia couldn't recapture that lighthearted joy. She was too terrified she'd fall.

"I'm not letting go." Jager whispered the soft assurance in her ear, nuzzling the black cashmere stocking cap he'd bought her in one of the glittering department stores lining Fifth Avenue. "I've been looking for an excuse to touch you for weeks."

Her attention darted from her wobbling skates to his handsome face. He'd been so good to her, helping her to tie up her work responsibilities at the McNeill estate in Martinique by hiring a temporary replacement. His younger brother Gabe—now technically her boss—had given her a surprise holiday bonus that was based on revenue growth for the property. It had given her enough of a financial cushion that she could send the money home to her father to pay the taxes on their small piece of land and keep it safe for another year.

Which was a huge worry off her mind.

Each day for almost two weeks, Jager had asked how she felt, asked what he could do to help make her life easier so she could focus on her health. She'd been touched, especially in light of the pregnancy worries she'd had—at least up until today's call from Dr. Ruiz. And more than anything, she appreciated that he'd given her time to come to terms with being pregnant, without pressuring her about marriage.

That window of time had ended, however. He'd made that clear in the car ride from the airport when he said he wanted to be with her again. That exchange was never far from her mind even as they were sightseeing and enjoying all the Christmas hubbub of New York City just days before the big holiday.

"Are you trying to distract me so I don't fall?" she asked, her heartbeat skipping to its own crazy rhythm.

The scent of roasted chestnuts spiced the air. As the music shifted to an orchestra arrangement of Handel's *Messiah*, Jager swayed on his skates, effortlessly gliding backward so she could remain facing forward.

"I'm one-hundred-percent sincere about wanting to touch you." The look in his blue eyes sent a wave of heat through her, warming her from the inside out. "But if it helps to keep you distracted, I can share some more explicit thoughts I've been having about you."

She swallowed around a suddenly-dry throat. The sounds, the scents, the night fell away until her world narrowed to only him. Her heart thumped harder.

"I don't want to get so distracted I fall on my face." She was only half kidding. Too much flirting with Jager could be dangerous. "But maybe if you told me just one thing."

Because she had a major weakness where he was concerned.

"Wait until we turn this corner," he cautioned, slowly drawing her body against his while he guided them around the end of the rink in a wide curve.

Pressed against Jager's formidable body, Delia didn't move. She didn't even dare to breathe since breathing would mold her breasts even tighter to his chest. Their wool coats and winter clothes didn't come close to hiding the feel of the bodies beneath. His thigh grazed hers as he skated backward, hard muscle flexing.

She felt a little swoony and knew it wasn't just the skates keeping her off balance.

"There." He checked the skating lane as he moved onto the straightaway for another slow circle around the rink. "You're doing well."

He loosened his hold without letting go and her skates seemed to follow him without any help from her.

"I'm not sure that not falling is synonymous with doing well." Her voice was breathless, a barely there scrape of sound after the close encounter with the sexy father of her future child.

"So we'll get right back to distraction tactics." He slowed his pace again, letting her close the small gap between them before he lowered his voice. "Do you want me to tell you how sexy you are in the dreams where you pull a pin out of your hair and it all comes spilling down while you straddle me—"

"No." She shook her head, unprepared for the details he seemed only too happy to share. "That is, not here."

He lifted a hand to her cheek and rubbed a thumb along her jaw. "Seeing you blush might be the sexiest thing ever."

"I'm just not used to hearing things like that from the same man who used to demand the Monday morning business briefs by five o'clock the Friday before."

He threw his head back and laughed. "I knew you were secretly opposed to those."

She liked making him smile, something that happened more rarely this year after tragedy had struck his family. Out of the corner of her eye, she saw Santa and a pretty elf walking through the brightly lit café that flanked one end of the skating rink. A family with small children posed for a photo with them.

"Employees want to be out the door at five o'clock on Fridays, not planning for Mondays." She'd been committed to the job though, and to improving herself. She'd never complained.

"I didn't keep you late *every* week." Jager loosened his hold a bit more, but it was okay since she felt steadier on her feet now.

"Only most Fridays," she teased. Despite their light banter, she kept seeing the dream image he'd planted in her mind.

Her. Straddling him.

She might not stop blushing for days at this rate.

"Then I have a lot to make up for." He drew her near once more so they could navigate another turn. "I hope this trip will be something special that you'll never forget."

"It already is." She lifted her hand from his neck long enough to gesture at the impressive ninety-foot Christmas tree covered in lights above them. "I've always wanted to travel, and New York is…magic."

Certainly, she'd never had a Christmas like this. The holiday had never been easy with her father the fisherman making little effort to spend the day at home most years, let alone play Santa or give special gifts the way other fishing families did.

"I've flown in and out of this city so many times for business, but I will admit I've never had as much fun as seeing it with you."

Her first thought was to argue with him—to call him out on a line meant to romance her. But hadn't he pointed out that he'd never given her a reason to doubt his honesty and sincerity with her?

It was her insecurity that made her not want to believe him. The doubts she felt weren't his fault. If she was going to make this relationship work, with a balanced approach to shared parenting of a child, she needed to start laying the groundwork for trust. More than that, she needed to start trusting herself.

"This has been one of the most fun days of my whole life," she told him honestly.

The fairy-tale images painted on her walls weren't all that different from this—the twinkling lights combined with the myth and magic of New York. In fact, the statue of Prometheus in Rockefeller Center was staring down at her right now, his gilded facade reflecting all the glow.

"Look at you," Jager observed quietly, making her realize she'd been quiet a long time.

"What?" Blinking through the cloudy fog of worries for the future, she peered up into his eyes.

"You're skating."

She glanced down at her feet to confirm the surprising news. Jager still held her, true. But she was gliding forward under her own power, the motion subtle but definite.

Happiness stole through her. She wasn't going to count on Jager being there for her forever. Not yet, anyway. This Christmastime trip would help her decide if he wanted her for herself, not just for the sake of their child.

But no matter what happened for them romantically, she realized that this man had given her a precious gift no one else ever had. He'd believed in her from the moment they met, giving her the courage to have more faith in herself too.

Whatever the future held, she was strong enough to handle it. To move forward. Even if it was on her own.

Nine

Later that night, Delia turned off the gold-plated faucet in the bathroom of their suite at The Plaza.

Gold-plated faucets. Twenty-four-karat gold, in fact, according to the detailed description she'd read in a travel review on her phone while she soaked in the tub.

After toweling off, she shrugged into a white spa robe embroidered with the hotel crest. Everything about the legendary property was beautiful, from the lavish holiday decorations throughout to the tiled mosaic floor in the bathroom. Delia took mental notes, knowing she could upgrade some of their offerings at McNeill Meadows when they hosted private parties and corporate retreats in the public portion of the historic house.

After padding from the bathroom into her bedroom, she scanned the contents of the spacious wood-paneled closet with built-in drawers. The butler service had unpacked for them while they were out sightseeing; her nightgown was neatly folded with the lavender sachet she'd packed on top of it. Even her scarves and mittens were folded.

Dispensing with the spa robe, she dressed in her own nightdress, a wildly romantic gown that had been a rare splurge purchase after her first raise. It was probably the kind of thing a bride wore—diaphanous lemon yellow layers with a satin ribbon through the bodice that tied like a corset. Although it was as romantic as any of her fairy-tale paintings, knowing that she'd acquired it through her own hard work always made her feel like a queen when she wore it. She'd come a long way from the girl who'd nearly bartered her future for a slick businessman who said pretty words but didn't really love her.

Switching off the light, she stepped quietly back out into the living room to admire the view of Central Park. She'd already said good-night to Jager, refusing his offer of room service for a bedtime snack.

She had the distinct impression he was trying to fatten her up, feeding her at every opportunity.

"Did you change your mind about a meal?"

The voice from a dark corner of the room nearly made her jump out of her skin.

"Oh!" Startled, she took a step back, heart racing even though she recognized Jager's voice right away. "You scared me."

"Sorry." He unfolded himself from the chair near the window, a tall shadow that became more visible as he stood in front of the ambient light from the street and the park below. "I thought you saw me."

"No." She became very aware of her nakedness under the nightgown. She hadn't even bothered with underwear, an oversight that made her skin tingle with warmth. "I didn't realize you were still awake."

"I ordered room service while you were in the bath. Just in case." He moved toward the wet bar, where she could see a tray of bread, cheeses and fruits. A champagne bucket held two large bottles of sparkling water chilling on ice.

She was tempted.

Seeing him tempted her even more. She remembered how he'd felt against her in the water that day he'd saved the drowning girl. The way they'd moved together later that same night when desire had spun out of control. She cleared her throat and tried to block out the memories of how his hands felt on her naked skin.

"That was thoughtful of you. Thank you." She reached for a water to quench her sudden thirst; her throat had gone very dry.

"Here, let me." He moved behind the bar, retrieving two crystal glasses. "Do you want me to switch the lights back on?"

"No," she blurted, immediately thinking about the lightweight nature of her nightgown. "We can see the view better this way. That's why I came out here."

While he poured their drinks, Delia walked to the window near the sofa and stared out into the night. The sounds of the city drifted through the closed windows. Horns, brakes, a distant siren provided a kind of nighttime white noise, the unique city sounds all muffled though, since their room was on the eighteenth floor.

Behind her, she heard rustling. Something heavy scraping across the floor. When she turned, she saw Jager had pivoted the couch to face the window, keeping the low coffee table in front of it.

"Come. Have a seat." He was placing the cheese board on the table, no doubt to tempt her. "We can see for ourselves if this is the city that never sleeps."

The invitation sent pleasurable shivers along her skin as if he'd touched her. The sensation was so vivid she debated scurrying back into her room with her glass of water and half a baguette to prevent a rash decision fueled by this insane chemistry. But running away from him every time this man enticed her was not going to lead to productive parenting for their child.

She bit the inside of her cheek to steel herself, then joined him on the sofa.

He'd never had to work so hard to win a woman's trust before. The way Delia's chin was tilted up and her shoulders were thrown back gave her the look of someone stepping into battle rather than just sharing a couch with him.

As she settled onto the tufted blue cushion, she tucked her bare feet beneath her, her sheer yellow nightgown draping over the edge. His brain still blazed from the way she'd looked while standing in front of the window a moment ago. There'd been just enough light coming through to outline her curves.

Her absolute nakedness underneath.

That vision would be filed away in his memory for a lifetime.

"I love how the lights run in a perfect straight line up either side of the park." Her attention was on the view and not him, her face tipped into the dull golden light spilling through the window. "It's so pretty here."

"You didn't mind the cold today?" He focused on slicing the fresh baguette to keep from thinking about touching her.

"Not one bit. I felt energized. More alive." She reached for a piece of kiwi and dropped it on a small plate. "I can't believe how much we did today after we landed."

"I think the cold makes you want to move faster to keep warm." She'd looked adorable in that hat he bought her.

She'd told him it was one of the most fun days she could remember, and it had been for him too. He'd never been the kind of guy to cut loose; he was always aware of his responsibility as the oldest brother in a family with no father. And later, no mother.

With Delia, it was different.

"Maybe that's the secret to New York ambition." She added a few more pieces of fruit to the pile, then extended the china toward him for a slice of bread.

"Frigid temperatures?" He layered on multiple pieces of bread and cheese before she pulled the plate back.

"Could be." Her smile faded as she peered out the window into the darkened park. "I never got to ask you much about what it was like to live out on the West Coast. Did you like it there?"

The question chilled him far more than the northeast winds had during their sightseeing. Perhaps some of his reluctance to talk about it showed on his face, because Delia spoke up again.

"We don't have to talk about that time, if you don't want." She chased a slice of cheese around the dish with her bread. "I was just curious how California compared to New York, since it's my first time out of Martinique."

He was never going to put her more at ease if he didn't share some part of himself that wasn't business-related. She knew plenty about his work life. But he'd kept many of the details of what he and his brothers had been through private.

"At first, I was excited to return to California since I'd lived near LA until I was thirteen." He'd been happy enough there, until he understood how unhappy his mother was. Until it occurred to him how his father never visited them anymore, abandoning his illegitimate family for his legal wife and kids.

"That's when your mom decided to ditch Liam and start over somewhere he couldn't find her."

"Right." Jager ground his teeth, the impulse to keep the past on lockdown stronger than he'd realized. He set down his plate and refilled their water glasses to give himself something to occupy his hands. "She'd had enough with his sporadic visits and she knew by then that he'd never leave his wife and other sons."

"Did you know about them back then?" She set aside her plate to lift the heavy crystal goblet. "Your father's other family?"

He studied the way her lips molded around the glass to distract himself from the old anger he always felt thinking about Liam McNeill.

It had been one thing to abandon his kids. Abandoning the mother of his children? Jager found it unforgivable, especially since their mother had fought cancer and died without a partner by her side. Just three devastated sons.

"Not really. As a kid, I had the idea that Liam had another girlfriend and that's why he didn't stay with us more." Remembering the confusion of those years, he had to give his mother a lot of credit for what she'd done when she left the country. "Before she died, Mom told us everything—about Liam's connection to McNeill Resorts, about his other family.

But by then, we hated him for not being there when she was battling cancer. We all agreed after she was gone that we didn't want anything to do with him."

"I can't imagine how hard that must have been for all of you." Delia bit her lip for a moment before continuing, "Liam never knew though, did he? About your mom's illness?"

"No. But keep in mind he lied to two women for over a decade, pretending to his wife that he was faithful and pretending to my mother—at first—that he was a single man, and later that he would leave his marriage for her." Much later, he'd heard that Liam's wife left him shortly after Jager's mother, Audrey, decided to end their affair. So he'd been free. He could have come for his other family, married his mistress if he'd wanted. But he'd never even bothered to search for them.

"After my own experience being deceived, I know that must have hurt both of them deeply." Delia placed the water goblet on the glass coffee table. The soft glow of light from the window played over her delicate features.

"I'll never forgive him," he told her truthfully, unwilling to give her false expectations for their visit. "I'm in New York to meet my grandfather, because I respect that it's important to you that we know my family."

On an intellectual level, he understood that it wasn't Malcolm's fault that Liam had wronged his mother. But Jager couldn't help feeling a sense of disloyalty to his mother for setting foot in Liam's world.

"It is important to me." Her eyes widened as she reached out to lay her hand on his forearm. "But maybe once you reconnect with Liam, you'll feel differently."

"Impossible." Jager knew his own heart, and it was cold where his father was concerned. Still, he regretted his quick response when her hand slid away. Swiftly, he changed the subject before she pursued the topic any further. "But you asked about life in Los Altos Hills. I was looking forward to it when I first got there last year, but after the hell Damon went through soon afterward, I don't think I could ever live on the West Coast again."

His sister-in-law had vanished without a trace after her honeymoon. Damon had punched holes in most of the walls of that big, beautiful home he'd built. Then he'd left town and shut off all means of communication.

Delia smoothed the embroidered satin cuff of her nightgown with one hand, fingering the embellishments stitched in pale blue thread. A placket on the bodice covered her breasts, while two layers of something gauzy and thin created a barely there barrier between his eyes and the rest of her. The urge to touch her had been strong all day, but now—remembering the way Damon's life was falling apart without his wife—the need for Delia was even more fierce.

"I've always wanted to see the Pacific." She had a faraway look for a moment before turning back to him. "Maybe it has to do with being a fisherman's daughter, but I'm more curious about the water than the land."

"I couldn't see the Pacific from the house Damon built in the hills, but the view of San Francisco Bay was impressive."

"There's a lot about the McNeill lifestyle that's impressive," she noted drily, straightening.

It was a welcome change of subject.

"We've been fortunate financially," he admitted, wondering how he could tempt her into eating some more. To keep her strength up. "But I hope you know I'd trade it all to see Damon happy again. Hell. I'd trade it all to *see* him." Jager worried about him. Damon wasn't himself when he'd left.

Jager grabbed the white china plate Delia had set aside and refilled it. It might not be a high-risk pregnancy, but she still needed to take care of herself. He'd read online that exhaustion would kick in over the next few weeks and she could lose her appetite even more.

"I wonder where he went?" She frowned down at the plate as he handed it to her, but she took a raspberry and popped it in her mouth. "Do you think he had a plan?"

"I think he was going to look for Caroline himself. Visit places her credit card was used in the last year. I spoke briefly to the investigator Cameron told us about—the one who said he could find Damon. But ultimately, I know my brother wants to find the men responsible for his wife's disappearance."

"That sounds dangerous. Can you stop him?" Delia set her plate aside again, worry etched in her features. Damn it. He hadn't meant to upset her. "Before he does something rash?"

He hesitated. The truth would only make her more uneasy. But Delia had been lied to before. He had no option besides being completely forthright.

"I'm not sure I'd want to, even if I could." The police had honored a request from Caroline's father that they "respect his daughter's wish for privacy." But Jager didn't believe for a moment that she'd left by her own free will, and neither did Damon.

Unfolding herself from the couch cushion, Delia rose to her feet. Clearly agitated, she paced around the sofa before returning to the window.

"But he could get in serious trouble." She laid a hand on the back of Jager's. "I didn't have time to get to know Damon very well before you all left Martinique, but I spoke with him often enough to realize he's a good person. If you could talk to him, you could convince him to speak to the police again."

Jager came to his feet, wishing he had more comfort to offer her. But his words were unlikely to ease her mind.

"Men came into his house. Took the woman he loved. And, as far as we can tell, those same men let her die alone at sea rather than return her to him after he did everything they asked." Talking about it made him agitated. Putting himself in Damon's shoes lit a fiery rage inside him. "If someone hurt you, I'd turn over heaven and earth to find them too. How can I blame my brother for doing the same?"

His heart slugged hard as he wrapped his arms around her, drawing her close.

"What if he finds the men he's searching for? He could get hurt. Or killed. Or end up in prison for the rest of his life if he—" Delia objected.

He gently quieted the torrent of worries with a finger on her lips.

"He's already suffering more than we can imagine. I'm not sure there's any punishment worse than what he's going through right now."

When she sighed, her shoulders sagging, he shifted his finger away from her soft mouth, feeling his way along her smooth cheek. His hand traveled down her warm neck to the curve of her collarbone, mostly bare above the square neck of her nightgown.

"Damon's in hell." The truth had been apparent to Jager when they parted. "He may never have the chance to touch his wife this way again."

He meant to comfort Delia somehow, but as he glanced up into her hazel eyes, he wondered if he was the one who needed the warmth of this connection. The solace of her touch.

The vanilla scent of her skin beckoned him. Her hair, still damp from a bath, was beginning to dry in soft waves. And damn it all, no matter who needed who, he couldn't deny himself the feel of her any longer.

Gently, he tipped her head back, giving her time to walk away if she chose. But her eyelids slowly lowered, her lashes a dark sweep of fringe fluttering down. He kissed her there. One press of his lips to the right eye. One press of his lips to the left.

Her raspberry-scented breath teased his cheek in a soft puff of air. Her fingers trailed lightly up his arm through the worn cotton of the well-washed Henley shirt that he'd pulled on along with a pair of sweats after his shower. The light, tentative feel of her hands on him seared away the conversation they'd been having. All he cared about was touching her.

Tasting her.

Cradling her face in his hands, he waited for her eyes to open again. He wanted to see acceptance there. When her entranced gaze found his, there was more than just acceptance. He saw hunger. A need as stark as his own.

Ten

Delia's world tilted sideways, her breath catching as she stared up into the laser focus of Jager's blue eyes. She felt herself falling and she was powerless to stop it.

If this night had been just about passion, maybe she could have walked away. But she'd glimpsed Jager's heart tonight, and the stark emotions she'd seen there had ripped her raw too. As the self-appointed head of his family, he took his responsibility to Damon seriously.

How could she argue with him when he would one day give their child that same undivided loyalty that he showed his brother? The power of that devotion was foreign to her, and it took her breath away.

"Kiss me." She whispered the command softly, knowing he awaited her wishes.

The two simple words unleashed a torrent.

He drew her into him, sealing her body to his, chest to thigh. Sensations blazed through her. Her breasts molded to the hard plane of his chest, her heartbeat hammering against him in a rapid, urgent rhythm. He bent to wrap an arm around her thighs, lifting her higher so his sex nudged her hip. Her belly.

She melted inside, the hunger becoming frenzied. Imperative.

When his lips met hers, she speared her fingers into his dark hair, holding him where she wanted him. Every silken stroke of his tongue awakened new fires in her body. A nip to the right made her breasts ache. A kiss to the left caused her thighs to tremble.

The fevered urgency spiked higher. Hotter.

"Delia." He reared away from the kiss abruptly, his eyes blazing. "A kiss won't be enough." His eyelids lowered, shuttering the raw hunger she'd spied. "That is, if you don't want things to proceed—"

"I do want. This. You." Tracing the line of his bristly jaw with her fingers, she inhaled the musky pine scent of his aftershave, then licked a spot in the hollow of his throat to breathe in more. "Very much."

Returning his mouth to hers, he palmed a thigh in each of his hands, wrapping her legs around him. Never breaking the kiss, he charged toward the bedroom. His bedroom. The feel of his muscles shifting against her as he walked provided a sultry prelude to the pleasures she knew came next. Her silk nightgown was a scant barrier to the feel of him, and he felt every bit as amazing as she'd remembered from their first time together.

"I thought I dreamed how good this felt," she murmured, keeping her arms looped around his neck while he toed open the bedroom door and strode into the darkened interior.

His blinds were drawn, the blankets turned down the same way hers had been. He paused near the dimmer switch on one wall to turn a sconce to the lowest setting.

"It was no dream." Carrying her over to the king-size bed, he lowered her slowly to the center. "Although I've been reliving that night often enough when I close my eyes."

"Me too." The harder she'd tried to forget about it, the more often every touch and kiss replayed in her brain.

He stood up and dragged his shirt up and over his head. Tossing it aside, he untied the drawstring on his sweats, the waistband dropping enough to reveal his lower abs. And…more.

He wasn't wearing boxers.

Lured by the sight of him, she pushed herself up to her knees. Her palms landed on his chest before he could join her on the bed, and she held him there, wanting a chance to explore, needing to imprint the feel of him in her memory.

Hands splayed, she covered as much of him as possible, skimming her palms down his chest, then turning at an angle to line up her fingers with the ridges of his abs. His breath hissed between his teeth, but she couldn't stop until she tested the feel of his erection, trailing her fingers down the rigid length then back up again.

She bent to place a kiss there, her lips following the line of the raised vein.

The harsh sound Jager made was her only warning before he hauled her up by the shoulders. "You play with fire."

"I'm already burning." She reached for the tie on her nightdress, a single yellow ribbon that wound through the satin bodice. "I need to be naked."

His gaze dipped to her body, his hands tunneling under the diaphanous layers of pale yellow to draw the fabric up and over her head, bringing with it the lavender scent of the bath oils she'd used.

Jager set the gown aside and stroked her arms. Shoulders. Breasts. There was a slow reverence in his touch that made her heart turn over, stirring feelings she couldn't afford to have yet. Not with so much uncertainty between them.

So she wrapped her arms around him and dragged him down to the bed with her, losing herself in a mind-drugging kiss. He covered her gently, keeping an elbow on the bed to ensure he didn't put his full weight on her. But she wanted, needed, to feel the full impact of being with him. She kissed him harder and skimmed her leg up one side of his, snaking it around his thigh until she could roll him to the side and lie on top of him.

"You said you had a fantasy about having me here," she reminded him, rubbing her cheek on his chest, soaking up the feel of him. "Straddling you."

"The real thing surpasses it." He captured her hands and held them on either side of his head.

To make sure he remembered it, she rolled her hips against him for emphasis.

He reversed their positions in an instant, flipping her to her back. His move surprised a giggle out of her. When his erection nudged between her thighs, she gripped his shoulders, fire rushing through her veins.

"Please." She needed this. Him. "Come inside me."

"Do you want to use protection? I have it, but—"

"We're both clean." They'd shared medical records for the sake of their child. She shrugged. "And I'm already pregnant. Let's enjoy the benefits."

The last words were muffled by his kiss before he licked his way down to her breast, drawing on the taut crest. She arched against him, wanting more. Everything.

He came inside her then, edging deeper. Deeper.

He lifted his head to watch her, his blue gaze fixed on her eyes. She bit her lip against a rush of pleasure so sweet it threatened to drag her under. She tingled everywhere, her pulse an erratic throb at her throat.

Clamping her thighs around his waist, she let the sensations roll through her. Poised on the edge of an orgasm, she simply held on and let herself feel it all.

Jager. Pleasure. Passion.

When he reached between their bodies to tease a finger over the slick center of her, she went completely still. He felt so good. So. Impossibly. Good.

Her release rolled over her like a rogue wave, tossing her helplessly against the bed, having its way with her. She was so lost in her own pleasure that his almost took her by surprise. But his hoarse shout of completion let her know she wasn't alone in the powerful throes of passion.

She clutched him to her hard, her head tipped to his strong chest as she slowly became aware of his heartbeat. It raced faster than if he'd run sprints. She placed a kiss there, smoothing her hand over his skin gone lightly damp.

Closing her eyes, she waited for her breathing to return to normal, her own heart to slow. With the flood of happy endorphins running through her, she couldn't imagine a time when she would regret what they'd just shared. It was nothing short of beautiful. But that didn't mean she could simply allow an affair to continue indefinitely.

She needed to think about her child's future. About maintaining a relationship with Jager that would never put them at odds. Not for all the world would she subject her child to the kind of confusing upbringing Jager had, never seeing his father after his thirteenth birthday.

"Can I get you anything?" His voice broke in on the crowd of worries creeping up on her, his hand tender as he stroked her tousled hair. "Something to eat or drink before bed?"

"I feel like Hansel and Gretel in the witch's cabin," she murmured, exhaustion from their long day starting to take hold.

"Okay. Did I miss something?" He sounded so baffled that she laughed.

"You're trying to fatten me up, Jager McNeill. Don't deny it."

"I've been reading." He tried to fluff the pillow under her head without moving her, then he straightened the blankets as they untangled themselves. "You might experience extreme fatigue in the upcoming weeks. I want you to be ready for it."

Imagining this all-business corporate magnate on his computer doing Google searches of pregnancy symptoms made her smile. He would be a good father. Would she ever measure up as a mother with so little to guide her?

A nervous flutter tripped through her belly at the same time his hand landed there. Right where their baby was growing. Her eyes stung at his tenderness.

"I'll be fine," she reassured him. "And I think the fatigue is starting. I'm so tired all of the sudden."

It was true. Yet she also wasn't ready to think about the implications of what had just happened.

About how important it was that she get her relationship with Jager right. Because no matter how tenderly he'd touched her, she had to ask herself if it was really *her* who mattered to him.

Or was he simply honor bound to care for the mother of his child?

Once Delia had fallen asleep, Jager could no longer ignore the notifications on his phone. Or, at least, that was what he told himself; he wanted to let Delia get her rest and he was still reeling from their encounter.

He'd wanted her, that much was damn certain. Still did, even after sex that satisfied him to his toes.

But he hadn't expected being with her to rattle him this way. There had been something deeper at work between them than sex. Knowing the whole time that she carried his child had been powerful.

So maybe he scrambled out of the bed a little too fast once she'd dozed off. But there were a hell of a lot of messages and missed calls on his cell. He'd noticed them earlier, beginning shortly after Paolo dropped them off at The Plaza. Messages from Cameron, Quinn and Ian.

His half brothers were all looking for him. Apparently they'd been summoned to the McNeill mansion to greet him tonight, and he'd never shown. In his defense, he'd tried to warn Cam he needed to have space of his own in New York. And he needed to meet with the family on his own terms. On his timetable. Now, stalking around the dark living room, he debated whom to text first. Before he could decide, the phone vibrated again.

Gabe.

Jager clicked the button to connect them. "I hope you're calling with good news."

"What good news could I possibly have for you?" his brother drawled. Gabe was as unhurried in life as Jager was Type A. "I know better than to think you'll get excited about the new crown molding I installed in the McNeill Meadows gift shop."

Dropping onto the sofa where he'd sat with Delia earlier, Jager stared out over the lights dotting Central Park and the few low buildings that broke up the dark expanse of trees.

"This is the woodwork you were making?" He'd visited Gabe when he returned from Europe, wanting to update him on the search for Damon.

As usual, Gabe had been in his workshop in the converted boathouse on the small hotel property he ran. The Birdsong had come into his hands as a teen when the older woman Gabe worked for had died. Her family had fought the inheritance for months, but the will had been airtight. Gabe had renovated every square inch, bringing guests from around the world to the Birdsong. He'd either restored or handcrafted all the woodwork himself and quickly got a reputation as a master. Now he had more work than he could handle from businesses that appreciated an artisan's touch.

"That's the stuff." In fact, Gabe had started the project based on a long-ago memo from Delia, when she'd been trying to make over the McNeill Meadows gift shop into a more period-appropriate space. "But I wasn't calling about that. I wanted to see what happened today. Did Cameron have an update on Damon?"

Leaning back into the couch cushions that still held a hint of Delia's scent, Jager ground his teeth at Gabe's impatience. But then, he could hardly blame Gabe for wanting to think about something besides his personal life. Gabe's songstress wife had told him their marriage was over while pregnant with their firstborn. She'd abandoned Gabe—and their son—two weeks after giving birth so that she could pursue her career.

The only thing keeping the guy's bitterness in check was his eight-month-old son.

"I didn't go over there today." He pounded a fist on the arm of the couch. "I'm not going to start reporting to Malcolm McNeill's every summons, and the quicker the old man understands that, the better."

"You went all the way to New York because they said they knew where Damon was, and now you choose to get in a pissing contest to prove some kind of asinine point about how we don't need them?" Gabe's voice lowered, a sure sign he was angry. "We all want the same thing. Bring Damon home."

Frustrated, Jager closed his eyes and counted backward until he could rein himself in.

"They don't want the same thing as us, because they don't even know him. The only reason they're helping us is to flex their muscle and bring us into the fold."

"Dude. This isn't a mob family or something where they're asking us to be part of a gang or start offing their enemies." Gabe's voice broke up on the last few words, probably as a result of poor reception on the island. "They are blood relatives and they'd like to get to know us. It's not their fault Dad is an ass."

Jager had tried telling himself that before, but there was some latent protectiveness of his mom that he couldn't quite shake.

"Still feels disloyal." He didn't have to explain why. Gabe understood him.

"Mom was tough as they come, bro, and she would never hold it against them." Gabe sounded so certain. And he'd had a different relationship with their mother. He hadn't necessarily been the favorite. But the two of them had been alike in a lot of ways. They were more generous and kindhearted than other people.

But you didn't cross them.

"I'll go over there tomorrow." Jager needed to speak to Delia about it, and see what she wanted to do. "I promise."

She'd stressed the importance of meeting his family, and keeping that connection open for their child's sake. But did that mean she wanted to meet all the

McNeills too? If so, did he introduce her as his girlfriend? The future mother of his child?

He wished she was already wearing his ring. He had no idea how to tell her that one of the stipulations in Malcolm McNeill's will was that his grandsons had to be wed for at least twelve months to inherit their shares of the family business. Would she view that as him pressuring her? She had to know he didn't want any part of an inheritance from Malcolm, but then again, it seemed too important a detail to omit given that he was going to keep asking her to marry him until she said yes.

"I'll call you tomorrow for an update. If Damon is stirring up trouble somewhere, we either need to talk some sense into him or—"

"Or help him. I know." Jager disconnected the call, and quickly texted with Cameron to make arrangements for visiting the McNeill mansion the next day.

Still, he shut off the phone feeling even more unsettled than when he left Delia's bed.

He had a lot to do to make a more secure world for the child coming in less than eight months' time. Tomorrow, he'd see the McNeills and demand answers about his brother. But first, he needed to have a conversation with Delia about the future. Now that they'd renewed their physical intimacy, she must have recognized how strong their chemistry together could be.

They needed to stay together because he wouldn't

be the kind of failure at fatherhood that Liam was. More than that, Jager would never give Delia cause to feel betrayed the way his mother had been. He would be there for her. They could have a Christmas wedding in New York. At The Plaza, if she wanted, surrounded by all the Christmas decorations she loved.

It was a damn good plan. But as he slid quietly into bed beside the beautiful, vibrant woman who'd set him on fire an hour ago, he feared he didn't have enough to offer her.

He had homes. Money. More security than she could ever want.

Yet after hearing about her upbringing with her stoic father, Jager wasn't sure how to convince her he could provide the one thing she wanted most. She longed for love after not receiving it. Jager knew how it felt and understood the way it devastated you when you lost it.

Planting a kiss on Delia's bare shoulder before he covered it with the sheet, he closed his eyes and tipped his head against her back. She sighed sleepily, curling into him. Fitting there perfectly.

Somehow, he would make her see there was more real security in shared goals. In a strong relationship based on trust. And in chemistry that would keep them both satisfied for a lifetime.

Eleven

Sinking deeper in her soaking tub the following afternoon, Delia tipped her head back against the soft bath pillow she'd discovered in a gift package from the hotel spa.

From Jager, of course.

After sleeping soundly for ten hours, she'd awoken to a room service cart near the bed with a veritable breakfast buffet just for her, including two plates of hot food on their own warming stands. She'd also discovered an assortment of gifts lined up on the bedroom's bureau. Jager had gone out to do some Christmas shopping, but left her a note telling her to enjoy herself until he returned. How on earth had she slept through his departure?

She lifted one arm from the water to examine her fingers for their level of pruning and decided she'd probably soaked long enough. She emerged from the bath and stepped into the shower stall to rinse off the spa oils from her skin and deep conditioner from her hair, deciding the only possible explanation for her heavy sleep was the pregnancy. She hadn't experienced any nausea and her breasts seemed to be the same size as normal, so she hadn't felt many effects of carrying a baby. But she wasn't one to sleep so soundly or for so long, and even when she awoke she'd been heavy-limbed and a bit foggy.

The bath and shower were welcome indulgences after the big breakfast. Jager would have been pleased to see how hungry she'd been.

Of course, the voracious appetite might have resulted from the late-night extracurricular activity. She stretched languidly in the shower, remembering the feel of Jager's hands all over her. She was still hypersensitive everywhere, her body pleasantly warm and satiated.

Shutting off the spray, she wrapped herself in fluffy white towels and breathed in the heady fragrances from the bath oils and hair products. The spa package had inspired her to try some new herbal combinations when she got back to work at McNeill Meadows. She would also have to give a lot of thought to how she would balance the responsibilities of her job with the care of her child.

Returning to the spacious closet in her bedroom to choose an outfit, she heard rustling in the living area.

"Jager?" Barefoot, she hurried toward the door adjoining the rooms. Then, recognizing how eager she was to see him, she forced herself to slow down.

"Delia." His voice was teasing. Good-humored. Had he been as stirred by their night together as she?

Cracking open the door, she peered out to see him scoop up a small package gift wrapped in gold foil printed with red holly berries and tied with a red velvet bow.

"I got you a pre-Christmas present," he announced, approaching with the gift held out in front of him.

He wore dark pants and a white dress shirt she happened to know was custom-made for him since she'd been in his office one long-ago day when his tailor had arrived with a garment bag containing that season's wardrobe update. No surprise, it fit him perfectly, molding to his shoulders and tapering to accommodate his athletic frame.

She heated all over remembering how well he'd used that sexy body of his last night.

"That was nice of you," she offered after a pause. "I should dress first."

"Please don't think that's necessary on my account." He stopped just inches from the door but didn't open it the rest of the way.

Letting her set the pace.

"I'm not sure we should make a habit of this." She

didn't sound remotely convincing, especially since his nearness made her all hot and breathless.

"Of gift giving?" He arched an eyebrow, a wicked grin curling his lips.

Sweet. Heaven. She wanted his mouth on her.

She released her hold on the door, letting it fall open a bit more.

"Forget what I said." She tipped her head sideways against the door frame. "How about if I thank you for the present first, and then I'll unwrap it?"

His eyes narrowed. His nostrils flared. And he set the package aside on a narrow console table as he understood her meaning.

"That hardly seems fair, but I live to please you." He reached for her, circling her waist and pulling her close.

His woodsy aftershave acted like an aphrodisiac, calling to mind all the ways she'd kissed him the night before.

Having his hands on her only deepened her hunger.

"I do believe pregnancy is finally increasing my appetite." Delia grazed his mouth with hers once. Twice. Then she tugged his lower lip gently between her teeth. "At least one kind of appetite."

With a growl of approval, he bent to lift her off her feet and cradled her in his arms. He headed for the bed.

"It could be *me* that's driving the new hunger." His fingers flexed lightly against her, squeezing her closer. "Either way, I'm going to be the one to satisfy it."

Her eyes fell shut with the need to concentrate on all her other senses, especially the feel of him. The feel of his powerful body levering over hers when he lay with her on the bed. Of his hips sinking into hers, even through the damp towel around her waist.

He kissed her with a care and attentiveness they'd been too impatient for the previous night. He caressed her face, pressing his lips to her eyelids. Then he slid aside her towel to trail more kisses down her neck. Between her bare breasts.

Lower still.

Pleasure spiraled out from a fixed point inside her, sending ribbons of sensation to every hidden spot on her body. A trembling began in her legs before he laid a kiss on the most sensitive of places, taking his time, clearly in no hurry. Ah, but she was. Eager to ride the tension to completion. She saw stars and never opened her eyes, the pinpricks of light flashing a warning of the pleasure to come. He tasted her and she was lost, her hips arching helplessly against the sensual waves of sweet release.

He didn't let go until the spasms slowed and she sagged into the downy duvet, opening her eyes. Only then did he peel off his clothes and join her on the bed again, seating himself deep inside her. His presence there set off more aftershocks, and she wrapped her arms and legs around him tight.

He held himself still for a long moment, letting her

adjust to him. He stroked her hair, kissed her neck. And then he began to move.

She wouldn't have thought it possible to build the hunger again, but when he dropped a kiss on one tender breast, she felt pleasure swell for a second time. Seeing his perpetually shadowed jaw in contrast to the creamy pale skin there made her breath catch. Her nipples tightened more. Had she thought her breasts weren't sensitive from pregnancy? She almost shuddered with release from his tongue's careful attention to each peak.

But then he reversed their positions, letting her sit astride him the way she'd started to do the night before. Now, she didn't take the moment for granted, enjoying the way he let her take control.

She delighted in seeing what pleased him, savored the sensation of his hands on her hips, guiding her when he was ready for more.

And then he stole the rhythm back for them both, taking her where they both wanted to go until her orgasm broke over her. Her thighs hugged his hips, drawing a shout of completion from him. The muscles along his chest contracted against her palms and the knowledge that she pleased him as much as he pleased her sent a fresh ripple of bliss over her tingling nerves until, finally, she slumped against his chest, spent.

Cracking open an eyelid to peer up at him, she was taken aback by a sudden swell of tender emotions. She wanted to wrap her arms around him tight and keep him in her bed for days. She wanted to feed him. Make him smile.

On instinct, she shut her eyes again, knowing she couldn't let herself start caring for him that way. She hoped it was just pregnancy emotions making her so tenderhearted. When she thought she had a handle on her feelings again, she opened her eyes.

Unbelievably, the sun was starting to set again by the time her heart settled into an even pace once more.

"How can it be dark already?" she whispered against his bare shoulder, grateful for a neutral topic to speak about when her heart was beginning to hunger for a different kind of fulfillment. "I only woke up shortly before noon."

"I'm wearing you out." Jager frowned his concern, his blue eyes bright in the slanted rays of the setting sun.

"No. I'm just surprised how much shorter the daylight hours are here versus back home." She hadn't given much thought to it, but it made sense because they were so much farther north. "It's only a little after four o'clock."

He glanced away, and she could see his jaw flex.

"We're invited to the McNeill mansion for dinner tonight, but I will call them and reschedule."

She felt very awake then. A bolt of panic did that to a woman.

"Dinner? As in a meal with your brothers and grandfather?"

"I think they'll all be there, yes. Everyone but my father. They know my feelings where he's concerned." He gripped her shoulder when she would have leapt from the bed. "Delia, we can go another time. You're tired—"

"No. I want to go." She also wanted to look her best. To not embarrass Jager. "I was afraid you wouldn't invite me to go with you when you met them."

He stilled. "You're certainly under no obligation to attend."

Would he have preferred to meet them alone? She was torn between wanting to let him find his own way with his half brothers and wanting to understand the world her son or daughter would one day move in. Maternal concern won out.

"I want to be there. I just need a little time to get ready." She would assess for herself what kind of family her child would have.

She had so little to offer a baby in that regard.

"I'll leave your gift on the bed," he called after her while she hurried to her closet to find something to wear. "You might want to wear it tonight."

She heard the bedroom door open while she took stock of her half-dried hair. She couldn't deny a stab of envy for this baby she carried. A McNeill heir would be surrounded by more than just wealth and luxury, both of which she'd lived happily without.

Her child would have a large, caring family to love him or her, something Delia would never know. Even her father, never a demonstrative parent, seemed to have forsaken her. She'd been hurt by his reaction to her baby news.

She was having a child and, at the same time, her family seemed to be dwindling. Unless, by some chance, Jager McNeill started to feel the same new emotions that she'd experienced.

Christmas was a time of miracles after all, and tomorrow was Christmas Eve. Delia couldn't help a quick, fanciful thought.

What if Jager fell in love with her?

The question halted her, stilling her hand as she reached for a brush. What on earth was she thinking?

She had no business thinking those kinds of thoughts. The fact that the question had floated to the surface of her brain reminded her why it was so dangerous to indulge in a physical relationship. She was already falling in love with him.

Closing her eyes, she acknowledged the simple truth that complicated her life so very much. She'd hoped to use this trip to make a smart, reasonable decision. She was going to be a mother, a duty she took seriously. She couldn't afford to fall victim to foolish, romanticized notions. Again.

She wasn't here because she was Jager's girlfriend, or significant other, so she couldn't allow her new feelings to show. In Jager's eyes, she was simply the mother of his child. She would be wise to remember it.

* * *

"The jewelry is stunning, Jager." Delia fingered the diamond drop earrings shaped like snowflakes as she stood beside him in the foyer of Malcolm McNeill's expansive mansion in one of the most jaw-droppingly pricey parts of New York.

The maid who answered the door had taken their coats and then disappeared to announce them. Or so Jager guessed.

He thought he had been prepared for the family's wealth. But he wasn't anywhere near ready for a Cézanne in the foyer or the sheer size of the place in a city where tiny patches of real estate went for millions.

If the house caught him off guard, he could only imagine what Delia was feeling in her first trip outside Martinique. She was definitely in an unusual mood, something he'd noticed as soon as they'd settled side by side in the back of the chauffeured Range Rover his grandfather sent for them. Jager had watched her open the gift on the ride over, and while he was sure she'd been genuinely pleased, there was something reserved about her this evening. Restrained.

He hoped it was just nerves at meeting the more famous branch of the McNeill family.

"I hope the earrings make you think about how much fun we had watching snowflakes fall on the ice at Rockefeller Center." He kissed her temple just as the maid returned to the foyer, pulling his attention back to the impending encounter with his grandfather and half brothers.

"The family is waiting for you in the library." The older woman gestured to her right as she stepped out of their way. "The elevator is down this hall, and it might be easier than the stairs with your beautiful dress, ma'am."

"The skylight is so lovely over the stairs though, I wouldn't have minded a closer look." Delia peered up the formal staircase to the stained-glass window six stories above. She turned to smile at the woman. "I'll bet you see amazing displays of light depending on the weather."

"Some days are truly breathtaking." The woman nodded before disappearing down a corridor toward the back of the house.

"Speaking of breathtaking." Jager slid an arm around Delia's slender waist, careful not to wrinkle the silk taffeta skirt she wore while he guided her down the hall toward the elevator. "Have I mentioned how incredible you look tonight?"

She was vibrant in the ankle-length crimson skirt, a designer confection he'd bought for her with the help of a shopping service. They'd sent an assortment of outfits particularly fitting for the holidays and the long skirt with beadwork and appliqué was a festive choice. She wore a simple creamy-colored angora sweater with it, letting the skirt shine. The earrings went well with her outfit, dangling against her pale neck since she'd swept her fair hair into a smooth twist.

"You clean up well yourself." Her hazel eyes darted over his crisp white dress shirt and tie, as if scanning for anything amiss. She smoothed her fingers down the lapel of his black jacket and he wondered if she did so to soothe herself or him.

Either way, the caring gesture touched him as they stepped into the elevator cabin and he hit the button for the third floor. When the door closed silently, Jager picked up her hands and kissed the back of one and then the other.

It wasn't until that moment—halfway to the third floor—that he remembered he hadn't informed her about his grandfather's will. Swearing softly, he hit the elevator emergency button, halting their upward progress and making the cabin lurch awkwardly as it stopped.

Delia stumbled a bit, but he caught her against him easily.

"What are you doing?" Frowning, she righted herself by gripping the lapels of his jacket.

An alarm blared inside the car, a red light flashing inside the emergency knob.

"I forgot to tell you something important and I don't want you to be surprised, or think I was trying to hide it." He hated sharing it with her this way. "I meant to talk to you when I got back from shopping, but then we got so distracted—"

"Tell me what?" There was a flatness to her voice. An edge.

He didn't blame her for being upset. The flocked red paper on the walls around them seemed to close in as the alarm kept up its insistent wail.

"My grandfather is determined to bring all his grandsons into the business. To carry on his legacy."

She nodded, her hold on his suit jacket loosening. "I remember your half brother talking about that when he came to the gate the first time you and I were together."

"Right. What Cam didn't mention was Malcolm's insistence on his heirs being married for at least a year to inherit."

"Married." She pursed her lips.

He couldn't read her expression, but it seemed like the damn elevator alarm was getting louder.

"Yes." He tensed, willing her to understand it meant nothing to him. "I didn't want you to think that my proposal to you had anything to do with that. I don't care about the hotel business—"

"Don't you think I know that?" Delia shook her head, resting her hands on his upper arms as she faced him. Her words were reassuring but her expression remained tense. "I know you don't want anything from this family, Jager, but I'm glad you're at least in their home, hearing what they have to say."

He stared into her hazel eyes, trying to find out if he was missing something. "You're not upset with me?"

He would swear there was a stiffness about her

shoulders. Then again, maybe he was seeing trouble where there wasn't any. This damn meeting had him uptight.

"I'm a little embarrassed about what your family might say about our elevator mishap, but other than that, of course I'm not upset with you." She offered a tight smile.

He hurried to explain himself, knowing time was running out and not just because of the elevator. "You know I asked you to marry me because—"

"Because of the baby," she finished for him, straightening as her hands fell away from his arms. "Yes. I'm very clear about that, I assure you."

She pressed the elevator alarm button to set things back into motion again and Jager breathed a mental sigh of relief. She understood him.

And she said she wasn't upset with him.

So he wondered why she seemed to bristle when he touched her as the doors swooshed open on the third floor. He hoped it was simple embarrassment for the awkward situation, as she'd mentioned. He would do whatever it took to ensure this visit went smoothly for her. Because in spite of his grandfather's maneuvering, Jager had his own reasons for wanting to make certain he was married before the New Year.

Twelve

If Delia hadn't been upset about his insistence that he only proposed for the sake of their child, she might have been more appreciative of his anxious attempt to tell her about his grandfather's will. That had been kind and considerate, proving to her that he was a far different man than Brandon and—more important—showing her that he understood how hurt she'd been by her former fiancé's deception.

But instead of putting her more at ease for this first meeting with his grandfather, the conversation only brought home for her that Jager was thinking solely about social convention and his legal claim to their child. That hurt all the more tonight since she'd just come face-to-face with the realization that she loved him. And since she'd made it clear she wouldn't marry for anything less than love, his reminder that they should wed for the baby's sake only deepened the raw ache inside her.

Jager had asked her to marry him because she carried his child. It had nothing to do with any feelings for her.

The blunt truth hurt, but it certainly helped her to be less nervous about meeting the rest of the McNeills. She didn't need to worry about impressing people who would never be *her* family. She could focus on taking their measure because they would be her child's relatives.

"Seriously?" Cameron McNeill, the tall half brother who bore a striking resemblance to Damon, was waiting for them on the third floor when the mansion's elevator doors swished open. "Don't they have home elevators where you come from?"

"Funny." Jager extended his hand and the two men shook. "I figured the old man got wind there was an imposter McNeill in the house and hit the reject button."

"There are no imposters here." Cameron clapped him on the shoulder. "Although I'm more interested in your lovely guest." Expectant and charming, he turned to Delia.

"Delia, this is Cameron. Cam, meet Delia Rickard." Jager wrapped a possessive arm around her waist. "And she is special to me."

She swallowed back the automatic thrill that

danced through her at his words, his touch. She tried to focus on his half brother instead. Now that Delia could see Cameron more clearly, she realized she'd never again mistake him for Damon. Though both men were unusually tall, Cameron was probably on the high end of six foot four. And whereas Damon had been a serious man even before his wife's disappearance, Cameron seemed a lighter spirit.

"A pleasure to welcome you, Delia." He grinned as he squeezed her hand briefly. "And no need to worry. Now that I'm happily wed, I won't be issuing any more impulsive marriage proposals to the beautiful women I meet."

"I'm sure your new wife is glad to know it," Delia replied, remembering well the tabloid frenzy about Cameron's public proposal to the New York City Ballet dancer who later married Quinn—the eldest McNeill. Months afterward, Cameron had wed a concierge who worked for one of the McNeills' Caribbean hotels. The rush to wed made all the more sense in light of what Jager had confided. "And thank you for having me."

"If you're special to Jager, you're special to us. Are you ready to meet the rest of the clan?" Cameron held an arm out, gesturing toward the double doors flanked by carved wood panels at the end of the corridor.

The panels were the kind she'd seen in historic plantation homes, the sort of things that Gabe enjoyed restoring or even reproducing from scratch.

Grateful to have that first encounter behind them—and to have easily brushed aside the matter of the stuck elevator—Delia accompanied the men toward the library. She needed to tamp down the hurt and unease from her conversation with Jager mere seconds earlier.

When Cameron opened the double doors, she only had a moment to take in the richness of the room, with its walls fitted with historic Chinese lacquer panels between the windows overlooking the street. Quickly, she shifted her attention to the six other people she hadn't yet met.

Delia was glad she'd taken time to read up on the family—again—before the trip to New York, since the tidbits she recalled about the various members helped her to keep them straight. Ian was the first to step forward and introduce himself to her. Jager had already met Ian, the brother who was most involved in the hotel business, developing his own specialty properties in addition to his work with McNeill Resorts. Ian's wife, Lydia, a dark-haired beauty with deep furrows in her pale forehead, eyed Delia with an assessing gaze. She was dressed elegantly in a green tartan skirt and black silk blouse, and a velvet choker with an emerald pendant at her throat.

Cameron's wife, Maresa, perched on the arm of a wingback chair, composed and elegant in an ice-blue sweater dress that drew attention to honey-colored eyes, a shade paler than her deeply tanned skin. She was the only one in the group to hug Delia, a gesture that put her a bit more at ease for meeting the rest. Maresa no longer worked as a concierge for one of the McNeill Resorts hotels, but her warm manner made it obvious why she'd been so good at the job in her native Saint Thomas.

The last of the brothers was Quinn, the hedge fund manager who had married the exotic ballerina.

"Good to have you in New York," Quinn greeted them, his navy suit and light blue shirt conservative without being stodgy.

It was interesting to view Jager side by side with this man since each was the oldest of his respective group of McNeill brothers, and she recognized a similar way they had of sizing each other up. While Cam had been open and friendly, Ian was tough to read but warm, and Quinn, the oldest, clearly reserved judgment. That was Jager too. She'd seen it in business meetings.

She saw it in how he related to her.

He held back. He sure didn't rush to embrace people. He'd been as scarred by people in his life—the loss of his mother, especially—as Delia had been. Seeing him that way helped her to understand him better, even if it wouldn't change him.

"Good to be here," Jager replied, offering the barest nod of acknowledgment. "I hope to work more closely with your investigator while I'm here. Bentley."

From the back of the room, the gray-haired gentleman seated in a leather club chair—the patriarch himself, no doubt—finally spoke up. "Bentley will be here before dinner is served."

The crowd of relatives shuffled to give Jager and Delia a better view of Malcolm McNeill. His bearing commanded the room.

With all the attention turned toward Malcolm, the petite blonde beside Delia whispered to her. "I'm Sofia, by the way."

Delia glanced down at the speaker. So this was the ballerina Quinn had married. She was even more beautiful than her photos online, and she didn't even seem to have any makeup on. She certainly had a natural look, and her outfit was a simple black dress, long sleeved with a floor-length skirt that might have been severe on someone else.

Jager strode forward to shake his grandfather's hand, and Sofia continued to speak quietly. "Meeting Quinn's family was more terrifying than any audition I've ever had," she confided, forcing Delia to hide a smile by biting her cheek. "But they're not so bad."

Nearby, Lydia must have overheard because she softly chimed in, "When they're not brawling."

"She's teasing," Sofia rushed to explain, fixing her loose topknot that was slipping from its clasp. "Mostly."

At the other end of the room, Jager conversed quietly with his grandfather. Delia couldn't help but be curious about the exchange; the older man was smiling as Jager held out a hand to help him from his chair. Malcolm shook off the gesture, however, pointing to a silver-topped walking stick nearby.

When he stood, even with his slightly stooped back and bent knees, he was every bit as tall as Cameron. It was clear the brothers had inherited their grandfather's genes. He wore a smoking jacket, of all things, made of dark silk and belted over a pair of black trousers and wing tips. With his thinning hair still damp but combed perfectly into place, he had a debonair quality about him.

"My dear, I'm eager to meet you." His voice boomed the length of the room, and his blue eyes—that matched all the other men's eyes in the room—turned to Delia.

She swallowed hard, grateful for the reassuring pat on the elbow from Sofia.

Stepping forward, she braced herself to meet her child's great-grandfather.

"Hello, sir." Pasting a smile into place, she reminded herself she was good at this. In the same way that Cameron's wife had a warm manner from being a concierge, Delia had honed her skills making people feel comfortable at McNeill Meadows. She could do this. "Thank you so much for inviting me tonight."

Malcom paused a few feet from her, steadying himself on the cane. She wondered if his strength was waning after the heart attack Cameron had mentioned.

Jager might not have believed the story, but Delia

did. She guessed the older man's failing health had prompted him to act fast to unify his family.

"I am delighted to know you, Delia." Malcolm McNeill enveloped her hand in his larger one and kept hold of it. "You might have heard that I'm very committed to meeting all my grandsons and ensuring the McNeill legacy lives on through a strong family tree."

Family tree? Delia shifted her gaze to the floor, afraid her face would betray her secret.

"Gramps." Cameron exchanged a look with his wife and then edged forward to stand by Malcolm. "Maybe we should go in for dinner first."

"We haven't even offered our newest members a drink yet, have we?" Malcolm glanced around the room. "Lydia, love, would you bring me mine so we can have a toast?" He let go of Delia's hand to point at the half-empty glass by his abandoned club chair. "And for pity's sake, let's get Jager and Delia something." He nodded toward Ian.

Lydia hurried over to do her part, making no noise in her stilettos. How did some women manage that trick? She had a graceful walk that Delia envied. Delia felt more out of her element with each passing moment, and she most certainly would not have a cocktail to toast anything. Why hadn't she thought of that before she asked to attend this gathering?

"No need to wait on us." Jager beat Ian in his move toward the bar, a freestanding antique that held a few bottles of high-end liquor and three cut crystal decanters. "I'll get it."

Delia touched one of her snowflake earrings to calm herself. She had thought she wasn't nervous when she walked into the room, but Malcolm McNeill's reference to the "strong family tree" stirred anxiety. She felt certain Jager wouldn't have shared their secret with his grandfather.

But was there a chance he'd told one of his brothers? The way Cameron quickly cut off Malcolm's line of conversation made her wonder. Everyone would know soon enough, of course. But she wanted to discuss how to broach the news with Jager before they revealed it to his family.

"What would you like, my dear?" Malcolm asked her suddenly, fixing her with his clear blue gaze. "If Chivas isn't to your taste, there's a bottle of Tattingers we can open."

From the bar, Jager spoke up. "I know her preference. We're all set."

She could see that he'd poured tonic water into a highball glass with an ice cube and a lime wedge. Perfect.

Turning her attention back to Jager's grandfather, she saw the older man's gaze was fixed on Jager's actions as well. And was it her nervous imagination, or had everyone else noticed his discreet pour?

"You're not drinking this evening." Malcolm's observation confirmed her suspicion. He'd seen, all right. "Good for you, my dear." He patted her forearm and then accepted his glass from Lydia as she rejoined the group. “Very good, indeed.”

Could he be any more obvious in his implications? Delia felt her cheeks heat and remembered Jager saying how easy it was to read her because of those blushes.

“What did I miss?” Lydia asked, frowning as she peered around at the family.

The men tried to look elsewhere. Sofia gave her sister-in-law a quick headshake as if to discourage a follow-up question.

Jager returned to Delia’s side with two drinks, passing her the water before answering Lydia. “Only that Malcolm seemed pleased Delia isn’t much of a drinker.” He gave Delia’s cheek a kiss. “I think we’re as ready for that toast as we’ll ever be.”

Her skin warmed from the brush of his lips. She knew that Jager would have rather skipped the whole formality of a toast that put them at the center of attention. No doubt he’d only redirected the conversation to forestall speculation that she could be pregnant. It was kind of him, and yet the damage had already been done. Malcolm had all but shouted it from the rooftops in his own subtle way.

Unless, of course, Jager really had told his family that she was expecting without letting her know? That was hard to believe given the importance he’d placed on informing her about his grandfather’s marriage ultimatum. And yet, she already knew he viewed this baby very differently than he viewed marriage. The former meant the world to him.

The latter? A formality. Different rules might apply in his mind.

She found herself touching the snowflake earring again and forced her hand down to her side. Why should she allow his family to make her feel so uneasy? She might never see them again after tonight. Once the holidays were over, she'd be back on a plane to Martinique.

Around her, the assembled guests retrieved their beverages. Malcolm shuffled backward a step so he could lean against the sofa and set aside his cane. He lifted his tumbler, the crystal glass acting as a prism and reflecting light from the overhead chandelier. Jager's blue gaze landed on her with an unfathomable look. Did he regret bringing her here?

Jager tamped down the urge to tuck Delia under his arm and haul ass out of the mansion and the whole McNeill realm. Although Malcolm McNeill had seemed genuine enough in his words of welcome earlier, Jager didn't appreciate the way the older man put Delia on the spot. What the hell had he been thinking?

Clearly, she was upset. Jager had seen the splotches of color on her cheeks, noticed the way she fidgeted with her earring. He kicked himself for not insisting he meet the family privately first, but she'd surprised him with her emphatic decision to attend the dinner.

Besides, his number one goal this week was to make her happy, to change her mind about marriage so they could start building a future together as a family.

Damn. This was not helping.

His grandfather's hand—a surprisingly heavy weight—landed on his shoulder. "I'd like to propose a toast to every person in this room." The older man's voice rumbled with gravelly authority. "My grandsons and the women who stand beside them. I am proud to call you family." His gaze scanned each face around the library. "Tonight, we celebrate a joyous occasion, welcoming even more McNeills into the fold." He nodded at both Delia and Jager. "Cheers to you."

Jager watched Delia, hoping she wouldn't be too upset the toast made it sound like they were already married. Perhaps the family patriarch was referring to Jager's brothers when he mentioned welcoming *more McNeills*. But Jager could see her uneasiness grow even as she raised her glass along with everyone else during shouts of "Cheers!" and "Here, here."

Maybe he was the only one to notice the signs of her agitation. Her time dealing with the public at the McNeill Meadows property had given her easy social skills that hadn't been so apparent when he'd first hired her as an assistant. But he'd known her before she'd developed the ability to put on a public face. He spied the way she waited until she glanced down to bite her lip, hiding the sign of nerves.

The women in the group congregated around

Delia; he hoped whatever they had to say distracted her from this debacle in a good way. Quinn moved to speak to Malcolm, shaking his hand and complimenting the toast.

"I should have told you to bring an engagement ring with you to this thing," Cameron muttered in Jager's ear, his tone dry. "We've all been on the marriage fast track here."

"You warned me," Jager admitted, feeling more trapped by the minute. And they hadn't even sat down to dinner yet. "But I underestimated his commitment to his approach."

Cam sipped his drink, his gold wedding band glinting in the light, while he studied his grandfather. "I think when you reach his age, you say what you want and don't give a rip."

"If he sends Delia running, I'm done with him." Jager meant it. Seeing a tentative smile on Delia's face while one of the women spoke to her made him grateful to the females in the group. "I'm only here because of her."

She was all that mattered to him.

And, of course, their child.

It occurred to him that he thought about them—Delia and their baby—in the reverse order of how he'd been used to weighing their importance in his life. Ever since their first impulsive night, when he knew there was a chance she could be pregnant, he'd put all his focus on making plans for an heir.

But there was more to Delia than just her role in

this pregnancy, and he wasn't sure how to contend with his growing feelings for her. They were a distraction from the goal. An inconvenience that made him second-guess himself, and he couldn't afford that when he was so ready to close the deal.

Forever.

He had that engagement ring Cam mentioned after all. He'd been working on a Christmas Eve proposal she'd never forget.

Quinn moved away from Malcolm to speak to his wife, and Jager noticed Malcolm retrieve his cane. Jager strode over to intercept him, making sure his grandfather didn't corner Delia to press his family agenda.

"Thank you for the welcome." Jager leaned against the back of the couch beside Malcolm, thinking to keep the two of them separate until the meal. Or to change the subject of conversation.

But Delia was already moving toward them, her diplomatic smile firmly in place.

"It was nice of you to include me," Delia added as she came to face them both. "Even though I'm not family."

There was an edge to her words. No doubt, she'd been pushed to her limit tonight. Jager itched to take her hand. To kiss away her frustrations and make sure no stress touched her. No matter what the doctor said about her pregnancy not being high risk, it couldn't be good for a woman to be upset like this while she was expecting.

It should be a happy time for her.

"Well, I hope my grandson will change that soon." Malcom grinned broadly, unaware of the nervous energy practically thrumming through Delia. "I predict it won't be long until we have another McNeill wedding."

Delia's sharp intake of breath was audible. Jager put a placating hand at the base of her spine and felt for himself how tense she was. The room went silent. Jager drew a breath, prepared to make their excuses and depart.

Delia beat him in responding.

"We won't be marrying." She smiled sweetly, but her hazel eyes were filled with a steely determination he recognized.

He'd seen it the day she jumped in the sea to save a drowning child.

"My dear." The furrow in Malcolm's brow indicated that—finally—he understood he was out of line. Or that, at the very least, he'd upset his guest. "I only thought, since you are glowing at my grandson's side and you didn't imbibe tonight—"

"You were mistaken," she fired back, standing tall and proud and ready to do battle. "I may be expecting. But we have no plans to wed just for the sake of our child."

If Jager's future didn't hang in the balance of those words, he might have taken some pleasure from seeing this woman, once prone to being insecure, take on the intimidating Malcolm McNeill.

Instead, he felt a kick to the teeth. It reverberated squarely in his chest and every part of him. In spite of his every effort, he'd now be living out his father's legacy of bringing a child into the world without benefit of marrying the mother. That worried him.

But unexpectedly, the pain ran deeper, beyond losing out on a chance at a real family, one with Delia and their child. He was completely leveled by the fact that he'd lost his chance to win over Delia.

The only woman he'd ever loved.

Thirteen

Delia wondered if she would blame this moment on pregnancy hormones later.

It was unlike her to gainsay anyone, especially her host on an important night for Jager. But what made Malcolm McNeill think he could maneuver his family like chess pieces, especially after all these years? Is that what family was about?

In the heavy silence that followed her declaration, she became aware of Jager beside her. His face was a frozen mask she did not recognize. No doubt she had embarrassed him, and she regretted that. Deeply. But he could not have been surprised, as she'd already confided her deep need to marry for love. He, of all people, must understand that. He'd been there for her when she'd been falling apart from Brandon's betrayal. Jager had met her father and seen how that need for authentic emotions went back to her childhood.

Delia became aware of the deep, resonant ticking of the vintage grandfather clock while everyone around her seemed to grapple with what to say next. She understood the feeling, since Malcolm McNeill had put her in that precise awkward position from the moment he'd acknowledged her presence.

"I see that I've upset you, my dear." Malcolm found his cane with one fumbling hand and set down his drink with the other. "And I'm so sorry for that. You should understand I am accustomed to being far too abrupt with my grandsons about my hopes for the future, a flaw they have overlooked because of my age and my health. But that should not excuse poor manners."

When he reached Delia's side, he squeezed her forearm. There was sorrow in his eyes, and she felt contrite. For all she knew, he could still be manipulating her emotions, but she wished she hadn't spoken out.

"Perhaps we should leave," Jager interjected with a terseness that alerted her to how much this had upset him too.

Exhaustion hit her in a wave, making her acutely aware of the stress, the lateness of the hour and a sudden hunger. Her pregnancy hormones may have been late making themselves known, but these last two days had rocked her on a physical level. She felt a bit faint, her vision narrowing to two pinpricks of light.

"I may need to sit," Delia told him, done with caring about how well-liked she was among the McNeills. She'd been foolish to try to be a part of Jager's world. As much as she longed for family, she was not cut out for this.

As one, the McNeills moved to clear a path to the sofa. Jager offered her his arm and steadied her, guiding her toward the couch near the bar.

Ian's wife was suddenly beside her, holding her hand. "Have you eaten? Would that help?"

Delia nodded and someone, Maresa maybe, said, "I'll get it," and left the room. Delia let the soft hubbub of voices wash over her as her vision slowly returned to normal.

"It has to be stressful meeting us all." That voice belonged to Sofia. "Especially everyone at once."

"It's okay, Gramps." That might have been Cameron. "When I'm upset, it always helps me to clear the air. Say what's on my mind and then move past it. She won't hold it against you."

"Delia, would you like me to call for a car?" Jager asked in her ear, his voice kind and yet…distant. "You'd be more comfortable at the hotel."

"I'm fine," she assured him, her vision beginning to clear. "We can't leave now after I put everyone in an uproar."

"Your color is returning." She realized Lydia still

held her hand on her other side. Or, rather, Delia was gripping Lydia's hand for dear life.

"Sorry." Delia let go and sat up straighter. "I am feeling better."

"Maresa went to get you something to eat." Lydia lowered her voice for Delia's hearing only. "And we're excited for you, no matter what your plans might be. Babies are the best news."

Sliding a sideways glance to gauge her expression, Delia found a wealth of sincerity in those pretty green eyes. And, maybe, a touch of envy. Did Lydia hope to get pregnant herself? she wondered.

"Thank you. And I am very happy," Delia assured her, realizing how much more attached she grew to this child every single day. What started out as a shock had come to mean more to her than anything else in her life. Although, she had to admit, winning Jager's love would have come very close. Thinking about raising their child separately, losing the close relationship they had, made her heart hurt. But the notion of subjecting herself to a loveless marriage hurt worse. She'd been rejected enough by the people in her life.

Sitting beside him and feeling so apart from him was far worse than any dizziness and exhaustion she may have experienced because of the baby.

Maresa returned with a plate for Delia at the same time two servers entered with hors d'oeuvres for the group at large. The family all seemed as thrilled to see the food as her, probably grateful for a diversion after the tense start to the cocktail hour. Ian asked Jager about McNeill Meadows and the changes he'd made to the property to highlight its plantation history.

She breathed a sigh of relief as Jager allowed himself to be pulled into conversation. Hopefully they could get through the rest of the evening on a more positive note. She crunched into a cracker topped with warm brie and a slice of glazed pear, wondering how many she could devour without raising eyebrows.

As if reading her mind, Lydia winked. "Want me to find a few more of those?"

"Thank you." She nodded. "That would be great."

With Lydia's spot vacated, Delia had a clear view of her host in the club chair, which was situated at an angle to the couch. With both hands folded on top of the cane that rested to one side of his knee, he stared out a window, the lines in his face deeper with his frown.

Unable to leave things festering between them, she set her plate on the coffee table and slid down so that she sat closer to him.

She felt Jager's eyes follow her movement, but she knew what she was doing.

"Mr. McNeill, I began to feel faint while we were speaking and didn't get a chance to say that there is nothing to forgive." She patted his hands awkwardly. "You apologized to me, but I realize that I was unusually prickly, especially at what should be a wonderful reunion for your family. This is about you and your grandsons."

"It's about family. All of us." He shook his head. "I should not have been so forceful."

"But at least I could tell that you were enthused about this baby, and I'm glad for that." She had come here tonight, telling herself the visit was about her child when, really, she had wanted to be a part of Jager's world. To feel the embrace of a long-lost family. Did he know how fortunate he was to have people who wanted to claim him for a brother? For a grandson? "My own father has never expressed much joy in his family, so I may not be adept at navigating the nuances of…" She peered around the room, taking in the faces of so many McNeills, so many people who truly did care about welcoming yet another generation. "All this," she finished lamely.

"And I am so eager for family, I unwittingly push them away. It wouldn't be the first time." When the older man turned his blue eyes toward her, they were bright and shiny. "The mother of any McNeill is family to me," he said quietly.

Malcolm had spoken softly, but Delia could feel Jager's attention focused on them from the other end of the couch. He was listening. She hoped what his grandfather said meant something to him—at least in regard to his own mother, if not to Delia.

"For that, I thank you." The words certainly warmed her heart, even as they underscored all that she would miss by not marrying Jager.

"I had hoped to see all my grandsons married, so I put it in my will." He shook his head, bent in defeat. "Maybe it was not so wise."

She realized it wasn't just Jager who now strained to listen. Conversation around them had stopped once more. This time, Delia didn't feel the need to cross swords with him though, even though she guessed each McNeill in the room wanted to shout that his dictate was horribly unfair.

Yet it seemed to have netted three happy marriages so far.

"You might be better off letting your heirs decide what's best for their future," Delia suggested, reaching for her water glass before remembering she'd left it near her former seat. "Don't forget Damon already lost a wife he loved dearly. A dictate to marry again would only drive him away."

"You make a very good point."

All heads turned toward the open double doors to find the source of the comment.

Damon McNeill had entered the room.

Jager sat with his brother later that night in a second hotel room he'd booked for Damon at The Plaza. Between Delia nearly fainting and Damon showing up unannounced with Bentley, the McNeills' investigator who'd made good on the promise to deliver him, everyone agreed they would share a meal together some other night. Even Malcolm had been too stunned to argue, perhaps feeling abashed between his pushy tactics with Delia and then having Damon, quite possibly a widower at this point, overhear their discussion of the old man's matchmaking tactics.

Jager had had more than enough of the Other McNeills for one night. Cameron had let it slip at some point that that was how they referred to their half brothers. The shoe fit the other damned foot just fine.

Now, as he shared a beer and watched an NBA game with the brother he'd always been closest to, Jager realized his happiness at having Damon back was only dampened by Delia's insistence they wouldn't marry.

And yeah, it dampened his happiness a whole hell of a lot. Still, he was glad to have Damon's big, ugly boots planted in his line of sight on the coffee table while they watched a game being played on the West Coast. He needed this time to decompress after Delia's rejection. Decompress and regroup. He wasn't giving up, but he wasn't sure how to move forward to win her over. She was a confounding, complex and amazing woman.

"If we were still in Los Altos Hills, we'd be at this game right now," Damon observed, looking thinner and scruffier than he had in the fall before he left on his trip. He looked like he hadn't shaved since then; his dark beard hid half his face. "We left behind some good season tickets, didn't we?"

They'd left behind much more than that, but he wasn't sure how to broach the subject with his brother. Jager sucked at expressing himself lately, it seemed.

He'd fallen short with Delia when he'd tried his best to be honest and forthright with her—which was exactly what she'd said she'd wanted.

On the TV, a player went for a slam dunk and got rejected at the hoop. It was a perfect freaking metaphor for this day and the ring that burned a hole in his jacket pocket even now. He leaned forward enough to tug his arms from the sleeves and tossed the jacket aside.

When they'd arrived back at The Plaza, he mentioned wanting to spend some time with his brother, and Delia seemed only too glad to find her bed for the night. She was exhausted and happy to have a tray in her room, something he'd ordered for her before he left her two doors down.

"I waited around for you to come home," Jager said now, not sure how much his brother knew about events that had transpired in the past few months. "When I couldn't get in touch with you, I figured I'd better put the business on the market before it lost all value. You know how rumors of the founder's disappearance can make investors nervous."

"I'll take over with the business now. There's no need to sell." Damon clinked his longneck against Jager's bottle. "I just got held up."

Thinking about all the nights he'd been convinced his brother was dead, Jager set the beer down and sat up, barely restraining his anger and—hell, yes—hurt.

"That's all you have to say? After months of not

answering your phone and letting us all think the worst?"

Damon traced the outline of the name of the craft beer molded into the glass.

"I needed to find out what happened to my wife." His words were flat. Emotionless. "Unfortunately for me, I've come to agree with the police. She must have wanted out and didn't know how to tell me."

Jager was too stunned to reply for a long moment. Damon had been so certain she'd been kidnapped. "What about the ransom note?"

"Must have been a scheme for cash by someone who knew she disappeared. I still need to get to the bottom of that."

"You could have called. Or taken me with you. Or—" Jager shook his head. "You shouldn't have left us wondering what happened to you."

"Next time I lose my mind, brother, I'll try to communicate more." Damon tipped back his drink.

Jager stewed for another minute, hoping his brother would offer up the full story. Or at least a few more details. But he didn't want to push him.

Yet.

He'd find out what had happened soon enough. For now, he was so damn glad to have him back and wouldn't risk pushing him away again. There'd been enough screw-ups on that account tonight.

"So what's next for you?" Jager asked, wishing he had a wedding to invite him to. He would have asked him to be his best man.

Then again… No. He couldn't have done that. Not when Damon had been preparing for his own wedding just a year ago.

"I need to launch my software." Damon lifted his bottle to peer through the dark glass. He closed one eye and then the other, watching the TV through the curved surface. "Get Transparent off the ground."

"Sounds good." Jager liked the idea of Damon getting back to work. Before Caroline, he'd been able to lose himself in the business for months at a time.

Jager wished he could be on the West Coast for him. But he had already spent too much time away from McNeill Meadows. Would Delia keep the cottage if she didn't marry him? he wondered. But not marrying was unacceptable. Thinking about her pronouncement during the cocktail hour was driving him out of his mind. He needed to get back to their room and talk to her if she wasn't asleep.

And if she was, he needed to figure out a way to change her mind about marrying him and convince her first thing when she woke up.

"So." Damon set aside the empty bottle and glanced over at him. "You and Delia Rickard?"

"Yes." Jager ground his teeth. He had been irritated that his brother hadn't said much about where he'd been the last few months, and yet he realized he didn't feel like talking about how he'd spent his time recently either.

They'd never been an overly chatty family. And since their mother had died, they'd been quieter still.

"She's changed since the last time I saw her," his brother observed. "I almost didn't recognize her voice when I heard her from out in the hallway. She's feistier."

Jager had wondered what his brother thought about how she'd confronted Malcolm.

"She contradicted the McNeill patriarch all night long and still won the old man over somehow." Jager had only heard snippets of their conversation as they'd said their goodbyes, but he had overheard his grandfather wresting a promise from her to stay in touch.

The dynamic there was lost on him.

"Did they win you over?" Damon asked, pointing at the television and making the call for a flagrant foul a moment before the game ref did. "Are you going to be joining the petition to merge the families?"

There'd been a time when Jager would have simply barked a *hell no* in his brother's face. But maybe his time with Delia, thinking about a future and family of his own, made him view things differently.

"I think Malcolm is the only one who is psyched about it. Quinn was polite, but I got the impression he'd rather swallow glass than compromise the empire."

Damon chuckled, a sound rusty from lack of use. "I was there for twenty minutes, and knew in about ten seconds he's a carbon copy of you, dude. That's exactly how you look to the rest of the world."

Jager laughed it off to end the night on an easy note. Finishing his beer, he left Damon to watch the rest of the game on his own. He needed to check on Delia. Make a plan for tomorrow.

But as he strode through The Plaza's empty hallway shortly before midnight, he couldn't help thinking about what Damon had said. Did Delia see him that way? Uncompromising? Unyielding?

If he could figure out how to change her mind, maybe he still had a chance to win her back. Clearly, introducing her to his family had been an epic fail, but he had one last strategy that still might work. A plan he'd put in place before he even left Martinique.

Because to help Jager make his case to Delia, Pascal Rickard was on a flight bound for New York tonight.

Fourteen

Delia slept late on Christmas Eve. She'd been so tired and heartbroken the night before after the failed dinner at the McNeills; she'd forgotten that time was ticking down to the holiday.

And now, it was Christmas Eve and she was alone in her bedroom at The Plaza Hotel.

Through parted curtains, she could see snow falling outside. Fat, fluffy flakes danced down from the sky, taking their time on the way. Her first thought was to share the beautiful view with Jager. Until she remembered their awkward parting the night before.

She'd told his whole family they weren't getting married. She'd hurt him on what had to be one of the toughest days of his life.

He'd been cold and distant, barely speaking to her directly afterward. Of course, he'd had a shock seeing his brother walk into the library. She hadn't blamed Jager for wanting to spend time with Damon when they returned to the hotel. She'd felt deeply tired anyhow. But a part of her had also recognized that Jager was pulling away from her.

From them.

He'd said all along their chemistry was off the charts. He'd made no promises about having feelings for her.

Rolling to her side, she noticed the time—almost 10:00 a.m. *Wow.* She scrubbed her hand across her eyes. She'd slept half the morning away, the pregnancy sleep deep and heavy, as if her body needed plenty of quiet time to nurture the life inside her. Moving a hand to her flat stomach and touching it through the silk nightgown she wore, she marveled to think that her child grew there. One day, she'd be able to share the wonders of snowfalls and Christmases with this baby.

Or Christmases, at least.

Of the many things she would miss when Jager was no longer in her life romantically, snow seemed like a small, frivolous addition to the list. How many times a day would she think about ways she would regret not having him in her life?

As she sat up, her forearm crumpled a piece of paper on the pillow beside her.

Puzzled, she reached for it and discovered Jager's handwriting on hotel stationery.

There is a breakfast tray outside your bedroom. Please take your time getting dressed. I left an outfit for you as I invited a special guest I think you will want to see this afternoon. —Jager

Special guest?

She wondered if he meant Damon. Or someone else in his family. Key word being *his*. Not hers.

Although for a surprisingly touching moment last night, she had wanted to hug Malcolm McNeill tight for his kindness to her. She'd started off the evening so irritated that the older man had put her on the spot, implying she was pregnant when she hadn't been ready to announce anything. Yet by the end of their eventful time together, she'd felt a keen understanding and affection for Jager's grandfather.

Was it the overdose of hormones that made her so emotional? Or was she so hypnotized by the idea of a paternal figure that even Jager's bossy grandparent could win her over that fast?

Planting her feet on the floor, she waited for any sign of morning sickness, but she felt good. Solid. Padding to the door, she opened it and peered out to see if Jager was around, but she spotted only the silver room service tray, as he'd promised.

She also saw a huge, decorated Christmas tree in the living area that hadn't been there the night before. Red ribbons festooned the branches along with multicolored lights and ornaments that looked like…skyscrapers?

Unable to resist, she hurried closer, hugging her arms around herself to ward off the chill from seeing snow outside.

The ornaments were all New York themed. The Empire State Building and the Chrysler Building shone bright in the glow of tree lights. The Statue of Liberty hung from another branch, along with taxicabs, hansom carriages and even The Plaza Hotel with the flags flying on the front. Some of the decorations she'd seen at Rockefeller Center were represented, including the white angels blowing their trumpets and the gilded bronze Prometheus statue that presided over the ice skating rink.

The tree, the scent of pine that filled the room, it all mesmerized her, putting her in the holiday spirit. And outside in Central Park, that dizzying white snowfall coated the trees.

Had Jager done all this? Well, all this except the snowfall? Even a McNeill couldn't make demands of Mother Nature.

Delia wondered if this was his way of… No. She squelched the hopeful thought as she ignored the breakfast tray and jumped in the shower. She was unwilling to build up her expectations all over again. She would speak to Jager. Ask him about realistic goals for co-parenting in the future and plan accordingly. He might break her heart, but she couldn't afford to indulge that hurt. She had to be mature and responsible for her child.

No more running away from her problems on a Jet Ski.

An hour later, she finished drying her hair and dressed in the outfit she'd found on the lower shelf of the room service tray: a simple red velvet dress with a black ribbon sash. As if that wasn't decadent enough, there were red velvet heels with skinny ankle straps. Both boxes were stamped with designer logos from exclusive New York boutiques. And everything fit her perfectly.

She checked her reflection and wondered if it was wrong of her to wear the gifts after what she'd done the night before. Then again, maybe wearing the clothes was a conciliatory gesture. She didn't want to appear ungrateful after all Jager had done for her.

They'd been friends first. She wished there was a way they could maintain that friendship somehow. But there would be no going back now. Not after everything they'd shared.

Blinking fast before her emotions swallowed her whole, she braced herself for whatever awaited her in the next room. She thought she'd heard Jager return when she first emerged from the shower, but she'd done as he asked and taken her time getting ready for whatever special guest he'd brought. Fully expecting to see Damon when she opened the bedroom door, her brain couldn't process what—who—she saw.

Her father?

She blinked, but sure enough the vision stayed the same.

Pascal Rickard sat on the couch in front of the Christmas tree, a glass of eggnog in his hand.

"Dad?" she asked so softly she wasn't sure how he heard.

But he shifted on his cushion, turning toward her before getting to his feet slowly. Behind him, Jager rose as well. It was a sign of how stunned she was that she'd missed him sitting there.

"Hello, Delia." Her father placed his drink on the coffee table to greet her, but didn't move closer.

She looked over at Jager, seeking an explanation, something to account for this visit.

He cleared his throat. "I'm going to leave the two of you to talk." Jager grabbed his long wool coat from a chair by the door. His face was freshly shaven, but there were shadows under his eyes, making her wonder how late he'd stayed up with his brother the night before. "I told Damon I'd meet with him today about the sale of his company. Bring him up to speed."

She nodded, too dazed by her father's presence to think beyond that. When the door closed behind Jager, she moved toward her father, arching up on her toes to kiss his weathered cheek in a rare display of affection between them. But if he left his boat to fly halfway around the world to see her, she thought the moment warranted it.

To her surprise, he wrapped her in a hug with his good arm. She laid her head against his chest, noticing his clean new sweater and the heavy sigh he heaved.

She levered away to look up at him. "I can't believe you're here. Is everything all right back home?"

"Things are good. Better than good, actually." He pointed to the couch. "Let's sit."

"I didn't know you were coming." She dropped onto the cushion beside him, facing the Christmas tree that cast a warm golden glow on both of them.

Outside, the snowfall made the day feel cozy, the lack of sunlight making the tree lights more prominent in the room.

"I spoke to Jager last week." He picked up his eggnog and had another sip. Beside his glass there was a plate of sugar cookies shaped like snowmen that must have been delivered by room service. "He came back to town to ask if I would visit you here for Christmas."

"Jager." Of course that accounted for her father being here. He could have never afforded the plane ticket otherwise. "Why? I mean, I'm glad to see you. I'm just surprised he didn't mention it."

"He said he wanted it to be a surprise." Her dad's face had aged in the last few years—more than she'd noticed when they visited to announce her pregnancy. The weathered lines from his years in the sun were deeper, his pallor grayer. "I know I was surprised myself when he showed up. He apologized for being abrupt in the other visit when you both came to see me that day. Asked how he could help out. He said he wanted to provide for you and—for me too."

"That was thoughtful of him," she said carefully, not sure how her proud parent would view that kind of offer.

"It was a damn sight more than thoughtful," he grumbled, swiping a snowman cookie and crunching into it. After a contemplative moment, he said, "He offered to have my boat fixed and my roof patched. And made a deal with me and a few of my friends to provide the seafood for the Birdsong Hotel."

Gabe's resort property.

"He did?" She knew what that meant. Her father could take it easy. There would be no more stress about selling what he caught. Thinking about Jager doing those things for her father—for her—made her eyes sting with sharp gratitude. He'd never even mentioned it to her.

"I told him no—about the boat and roof, not about the seafood deal because I'm still a businessman and I've got bills too, bills I can now afford to pay." He pointed at her with the cookie, the half-eaten snowman taking some of the fire out of his emphatic words.

"But he insisted on the rest too, didn't he?" She already knew the answer. Two years of working for Jager McNeill had shown her that he drove a hard bargain. Weeks of being his lover, even when she'd been ducking his texts and afraid to face him, had shown her he was persistent and caring where she was concerned.

She was so touched. She couldn't stop loving him if she tried.

"Wouldn't take no for an answer. What's more, he gave me this passbook for a bank account with both our names on it—yours and mine." He dug in the pocket of his jacket he'd draped over the couch arm and then slapped a bankbook down on the coffee table. "It's got a balance in it already. Enough to pay the Rickard property taxes for years to come, so we don't have to worry each year about how we'll hang onto the land."

He sounded indignant. But also…amazed.

Her father, the stoic fisherman, had been bowled over by Jager's kindness. She was too. Yet she wasn't at all surprised.

"He's a good man." Her eyes stung more, as she wished there was a way for her to reach Jager's heart.

And wondered now if it was too late.

Had she been foolish to reject him when he had so much to offer beyond the words she longed to hear?

"I wasn't convinced." Her father passed her the tray of cookies. "Have you eaten? These are good."

She took one even though she craved the rest of this story more than the sweet. "What do you mean you weren't convinced?"

"I told him my daughter couldn't be bought." He set the tray down awkwardly, with cookies sliding every which way but somehow managing to stay on the plate. "You know what he said? He said you'd earned far more than what the land was worth doing a CEO's job over at that mansion of his. Any truth to that?"

A flutter of pride swelled her chest to hear Jager's praise. To know that he'd shared it with her father. "I'm not sure, Daddy. But I did run the property for almost a year while he was away."

No doubt about it, she still craved her father's approval.

"Sounds like a CEO to me." There was an assessing light in his eyes. "I told him my daughter and I are cut from the same hardworking cloth. You're like me in that we don't need a lot of recognition or praise. We just quietly get our jobs done."

Is that what he thought? That she didn't need to be told how important she was? Or special? New understanding slid into place.

"I think everyone likes to be recognized sometimes." She set her cookie aside, unable to eat until she told her father how she felt. If she could blurt out her feelings to a total stranger like Malcolm McNeill, surely she could tell her dad. "When I was growing up, I wondered some days if you even noticed what I did to help around the house or prepare the boat for your trips."

"Ah, kiddo," he said brusquely, shaking his head. "I bragged to everyone in town that I had the hardest working daughter for miles." He stared down for a minute and she didn't say anything.

Waiting.

Needing more from him.

"Delia, I know I wasn't the best father. I was already so damn old when you came along, and I missed your mother so much. Still do. It sounds crazy when I only knew her for a few years before you were born. I've been without her so much longer than I was with her. But I loved her so hard she left a hole."

The anguish in his eyes was the deepest, truest emotion he'd ever let her witness. And while she was grateful for the insight into her father's heart after a lifetime of wishing for his love, a flash of deep self-realization hit her.

She also understood in that moment why she couldn't walk away from Jager.

What if something happened to him and she was the one left with a hole in her heart? How much would she regret the time she wasted that she could have been loving him?

For that matter, maybe instead of worrying about how her father felt about her, she could simply share how she felt for him. She covered his hand with hers and squeezed.

"Thank you for sharing that. I love you, Daddy," she told him. "I'm going to be so proud to introduce you to your grandchild."

He closed his eyes for a long moment. When he

opened them, she saw a new tenderness there. "Love you too, missy. And I never did deserve such a good girl, but I sure am proud of you."

He wrapped his arm around her and kissed the top of her head. Delia let herself rest in the moment, in the gift of finally having a connection to her dad.

"Can I ask you a question?" She angled back to look at him.

"Sure thing." His gaze darted around, as if he was embarrassed by the emotion. When his focus landed on the cookies, he seized another frosted snowman.

"What did Jager say to convince you to come to New York?"

"He said he wanted to give you the best Christmas ever and he thought—for some crazy reason—that meant you might like to see your old man."

"He was right, you know. This is the best Christmas gift he could have given me." Well, one of the best. Having Jager's heart for a lifetime…that was something she couldn't deny she deeply craved and wasn't sure he could give.

But for the first time, she knew she had to risk it.

Her father shook his head. "I know I behaved badly when you told me about the baby, Delia. But you did shock the stuffing out of me when you showed up with that news."

She remembered the way he'd paled at her announcement, no doubt remembering his beloved wife who'd died in childbirth. "I was still reeling myself or I wouldn't have sprung it on you that way. I'm so glad you're here though."

"I got a new sweater out of the deal too." He rubbed a gnarled hand over the cream-colored wool. "It's a fisherman's sweater, you know. And I'll be damned but I never had one before." He flipped his wrist over suddenly to look at his watch. "That reminds me though. I made a deal with Jager to let him know when we finished our talk."

Straightening from the sofa, he reached for his jacket. So soon? She felt off-kilter from this day and it had only just started. But she'd already gotten two wonderful gifts.

An acceptance from her father she'd craved her whole lifetime. And a new determination to share her heart with Jager, no matter the cost.

"I hope we'll have more time to visit than that." She stood too, wondering what kind of arrangement Jager had made with her father. Apparently they'd been conversing often in the last weeks. "You just got here and I've been a neglectful daughter these last two years."

"Nonsense." He brushed aside her worry with a wave. "You had a plantation house to run, for Pete's sake. Besides, I've got some sightseeing to do today while you…do other things." He pointed toward the door. "I've got a room down the hall, you know. And tomorrow is Christmas."

She followed him to the door, the red velvet skirt

of her long dress swishing pleasantly around her legs. She'd worn the snowflake earrings too because it was Christmas Eve, after all, and the dress called for festive jewelry even if it was only noontime.

"See you soon then?" she asked, fitting in one more hug before he left.

"For sure. We'll see each other tomorrow. Merry Christmas, Delia."

She smiled, inside and out, to have a holiday to look forward to with her father. How many other Christmases had he spent at sea while she'd been at home by herself?

Peering down the corridor after him, she watched his slightly bent form and his wide-legged seamen's walk as he departed. He barely paused his stride to knock twice on a door down the hall. Damon's room, she guessed, where Jager was visiting with his brother.

Her mind swirling with thoughts, her nerves alight with apprehension, she ducked back into their suite, shutting the door behind her and pressing her spine to it for a moment while she caught her breath. Was Jager on his way back now?

And what should she say about last night and her public refusal to marry him? He'd arranged for her father's trip and the tree before the blow she'd dealt him in front of his family. Had she damaged beyond repair what little chance they may have had together? She wished she could take those words back.

All she could do now was not waste whatever time they had left. To make his Christmas as special as he'd tried to make hers.

Jager knocked before he opened the hotel door with his pass card, wanting to warn Delia he was here. Things had ended so awkwardly between them last night, so he wanted to be as considerate as possible.

Bringing Pascal to New York had been a shot in the dark, and he had no idea if the surly fisherman had mended his relationship with his daughter. But after hearing her dad's quick knock at Damon's door, Jager knew the time had come for him to face Delia himself. To salvage whatever he could of their relationship.

And while he wanted that to be marriage and forever, he was going to try to be patient. Hear her out. Understand her misgivings before he tackled them, one by one, to show her how good they could be together.

"Delia?" He didn't see her in the living area by the noble fir he'd ordered before dawn. The hotel staff had been excited to help him decorate while Delia slept.

"Coming," she called from her bedroom. "I'm just finishing up something."

"How are you feeling?" He laid his overcoat on a chair, noticing the flurries still swirling outside. It was picture-perfect, snow globe weather.

"Good." Her response was quick, coming a moment before she breezed into the room, looking so beautiful she took his breath away.

"You look…so very lovely." He couldn't imagine not having her in his life—as his wife. Not being there with her to share moments in their child's life.

"It's a gorgeous dress." She swayed slightly, a sweet, feminine movement that sent the skirt swirling around her legs. "I love how it feels."

"It's not the dress." He wanted to reach out to her. To hold her. "It's all you."

Her hazel eyes tracked his, as if she was trying to gauge his mood. He remembered what Damon said about how he was hard to read—like his half brother Quinn. So, digging deeper, he stepped closer. Picked up her hand.

She held a paper, still warm from the in-room printer. She set it hastily aside, making him curious, but mostly grateful that she let him touch her this way. He bent to kiss the back of her fingers.

"I'm so sorry for the fiasco at my grandfather's last night."

"I'm not." She bit her lip. "That is, I'm sorry that I got upset and blurted out words I didn't mean in front of your family. But I'm not at all sorry I moved past that and got to talk with them and get to know them. I actually think Malcolm is kind of great."

Jager hung on to the first part of what she said—about being sorry for blurting words she didn't mean—so he almost missed the rest. Did she regret her announcement that they wouldn't marry? Or something else?

He backed up a step so they could sit near the tree, bringing her with him and drawing her down to the couch.

"You don't mind that Malcolm rudely called out your pregnancy in front of a room full of strangers?" He started there, dealing with the less thorny question first.

The one less inclined to shred him.

"They weren't strangers though. But yes, I did mind. That's why I gave such a knee-jerk response, and I'm sorry for that. Very sorry." She squeezed his hand in both of hers. "Whatever happens with our relationship, I do think it's between us and none of their business, no matter how many wills and contracts he draws up to try to maneuver his grandsons."

"Whatever happens," he repeated carefully, sounding out the words like a kid reading his first book. Damn, but he was far gone for this woman. "Meaning, you haven't closed the door on a marriage down the road."

"No," she said breathlessly, before looking down for a moment, and when she met his gaze again, her hazel eyes were a brighter green, lit with some new emotion behind them. "All this time, I've been so determined to avoid a loveless marriage. But what I realized today, while I was talking to my father, is that a union between us could never be a loveless marriage. Not even close. Because I love you, Jager."

His chest swelled with love for her, even as he regretted he hadn't been the one to say those words first when he knew how much they meant to her.

Her declaration leveled every plan he'd made to win her back. Detonated the elaborate presents and gestures he'd orchestrated for the best Christmas. Because she'd just given him the most perfect gift of all.

"Delia. My love." He shook his head, scrambling to get this right without all the plans. To go off script for the most important moment of his life. "I have been planning for days to prove my love to you. To *show* you how I feel so that you would believe it, deep in your heart." Damn, but she humbled him. "Yet in a single moment, you showed me how powerful those three simple words are all on their own."

Her smile was happy. Secure. Certain.

"I was almost afraid to hope when I saw the tree. And my father." She bit her lip, but it wasn't nervousness. It was like she was trying to hold back her excitement before it burst right out of her. "Your gifts inspired me to take a risk on that hope and to give you something too."

She started to reach for the paper she'd set aside and he stayed her hand.

"Wait. It's my turn to give you something first." He withdrew the ring he'd had made for her. "Delia.

Love of my life. I would be more honored than I can say if you would be my wife."

Eyes wide, she gasped when she saw the ring. "It's a heart."

"You've had mine in the palm of your hand ever since the day you nearly mowed me down on a Jet Ski." He held the ring over her left hand, waiting for her permission to slide it in place. "It's only fitting you wear it here, where you can see it every single day, and remember how much I love you."

"Yes." She nodded, and then kissed his left cheek and stroked his right with tender fingers. "Yes, I will marry you, Jager, and be your wife."

As he slid the ring home, he realized he'd been holding his breath. She did that to him.

"I'm going to remember, every day, how powerful those words are," he vowed, so grateful to have her in his life and in his heart.

Forever.

"Do you want to see my present?" she asked, curling into him, her silken hair clinging to his cheek.

"You've already given me more than any man deserves. But I'd be glad for any gift from you."

She reached for the paper that she'd been printing when he walked into their suite. In the warm glow of the Christmas tree lights, he could see that she'd printed the application for a marriage license.

"I wanted to show you that I didn't mean what

I said at your grandfather's house." She peered up at him.

Jager kissed her nose. "You're going to be the most beautiful Christmas bride."

"Can we invite your family?" She straightened on the couch, so full of hope and happiness that he felt too.

"We'll invite *our* family," he assured her. "Every last one of them."

She wrapped her slender arms around him, and he wondered if she'd ever know how much he loved her. Thankfully, he had a whole lifetime to show her. Starting right now.

Epilogue

One week later

"You may now kiss the bride." The young, ruddy-faced justice of the peace closed his officiant's book and grinned broadly at Delia and Jager.

They stood side by side for their New Year's Eve wedding at The Plaza Hotel in the famed Palm Court, which Malcolm McNeill had bought out for a few hours to enjoy a private, late-afternoon ceremony. Delia wore a specially designed gown from an up-and-coming designer friend of Lydia's, who had fully delivered on Delia's request for a fairy-tale dress. Off-the-shoulder chiffon, fitted through the bodice and waist, the dress had a full skirt and short train worthy of any princess. Delia carried red roses and poinsettias, her heart-shaped ring firmly in place on her finger for a lifetime.

"My wife." Jager's quiet words, spoken as his lips hovered just above hers, gave the happy moment a power and meaning that she understood deeply. "My love."

The kiss that sealed their promise made her light-headed with joy. Or maybe it was the sentiment he expressed, since it was echoed in her own heart.

"Congratulations, Mr. and Mrs. McNeill." The justice of the peace's words called her back to the reality of the wedding day, and reminded her that they weren't just celebrating their marriage.

Turning toward their small group of assembled guests, Delia knew that promise she'd just made was also a celebration of family. A wonderful new chapter for all of the McNeills, who had taken the first slow steps toward making peace. Toward giving Malcolm McNeill the united kin he dearly craved.

She glanced his way now, and saw the happy tears in his eyes. He didn't even bother to hide them. He was the exact opposite of her father, who of course chose that moment to put his fingers between his teeth and let out a wolf whistle. Cameron McNeill seemed to like this salute to the new couple, and he did the same thing, filling the air with their whistled approval.

"I think that means they want us to kiss again,"

Jager suggested in her ear. He hadn't let go of her hand since they'd exchanged rings.

Or maybe it was she who couldn't let go of him.

"I think you're right." She kissed her husband again, for longer this time.

She kissed him until the room broke into applause and cheers. But soon decorum prevailed and her cheeks heated just a little.

Jager must have noticed, because he gave one warm cheek a kiss before he drew her over to the dance floor, where they had agreed to share a first dance as man and wife before a meal with the family.

"Shouldn't we thank everyone for coming first? Mingle?" Biting her lip, she peered back at the group seated under an archway of palms outlined with white lights for the holidays.

They hadn't spent a lot of time planning their wedding since they'd only invited family, but Delia was new to having so many siblings-in-law and she wanted to entertain them well. Do things right. Make sure they had fun.

"We'll visit with them soon enough." Jager's blue gaze was for her alone.

And from the heated flame in their depths, she knew he wasn't thinking about family.

"Then I guess I'll follow your lead, husband." She set her bouquet aside as the chamber orchestra began the opening strains of their wedding song.

"I wouldn't steer you wrong," he assured her, nibbling at her neck as they turned together on the small parquet floor. "I taught you to ice skate after all."

It was such a happy memory. And they had so many more left to make together.

"I trust you." She followed his steps, letting him guide her as they twirled past a waiter bringing in the wedding cake, which consisted of layers and layers of red velvet iced in white. She didn't need to see the cake to know the bride-and-groom topper danced inside a snow globe. She'd adored the magical romance of the pretty decoration, so fitting for how she'd fallen in love.

"Should we make New York a yearly trip at Christmastime?" Jager asked, and she guessed his thoughts were following the same line as hers. "We'll have to introduce our child to his or her great grandfather next year."

She couldn't wait for her second ultrasound appointment two days from now, before they flew back to Martinique. It was too soon to determine gender, of course, but she wanted to see their baby.

"I'll be surprised if Malcolm waits that long for a meeting." She'd had fun visiting with the older man in their two trips to the McNeill mansion since that dubious first meeting. He had been overjoyed at the news of the marriage, all the more so since he'd been afraid he'd driven a wedge between Delia and Jager.

"He is a family man, through and through," Jager admitted. He and Damon had agreed that they would try salvaging a relationship with this branch of the family.

Gabe, with his own child to consider, had been game all along. He was already in discussions with his half brothers about taking over some of the Caribbean properties.

"How do you think your brothers will fare with the marriage maneuvers?" She was worried about Damon.

He had stayed in New York to attend the wedding, but there was a deep sadness in his eyes even at happy times.

"They'll set the old man straight," Jager said with certainty as the closing bars of their song filled the room. "Malcolm McNeill might be growing on me as a person, and as a grandfather. But that doesn't mean he controls us."

Delia glided to a stop, peering over at the patriarch surrounded by grandsons who obviously adored him. Even Damon sat close by, listening intently to something Malcolm had to say.

It warmed her heart. But then, everything about this day did.

"I love you so much, Jager." Happy tears welled up, as they had all week, and she knew it didn't have anything to do with pregnancy hormones.

Jager kissed her, giving her a moment to compose herself. A moment to savor how perfect and special this day was.

"I love you, Delia." His words wrapped around her as surely as his arms. "More than I can ever say."

* * * * *

If you liked this story of the McNeill family,
pick up these other McNeill books from
Joanne Rock!

THE MAGNATE'S MAIL-ORDER BRIDE
THE MAGNATE'S MARRIAGE MERGER
HIS ACCIDENTAL HEIR

As well as reader favorite
SECRET BABY SCANDAL

Available now from Harlequin Desire!

***

And don't miss the next LITTLE SECRETS *story*
LITTLE SECRETS: UNEXPECTEDLY
PREGNANT
by Joss Wood
Available January 2018!

***

If you're on Twitter, tell us what you think of
Harlequin Desire! #harlequindesire

COMING NEXT MONTH FROM

Available January 2, 2018

#2563 THE RANCHER'S BABY

Texas Cattleman's Club: The Impostor • by Maisey Yates

When Selena Jacobs's ex-husband shows up at his own funeral, it's her estranged best friend who insists on staying with her to keep her safe. But living with the one who got away gets complicated when one night leads to an unexpected surprise...

#2564 TAMING THE TEXAN

Billionaires and Babies • by Jules Bennett

Former military man turned cowboy Hayes Elliott is back at the family ranch to recover from his injuries. The last thing he needs is to fall into bed with temptation...especially when she's a sexy single mom who used to be married to his best friend!

#2565 LITTLE SECRETS: UNEXPECTEDLY PREGNANT

by Joss Wood

Three years ago, Sage pushed Tyce away. Three months ago, they shared one (mistaken) red-hot night of passion. Now? She's pregnant and can't stay away from the man who drives her wild. But as passion turns to love, secrets and fears could threaten everything...

#2566 CLAIMING HIS SECRET HEIR

The McNeill Magnates • by Joanne Rock

Damon McNeill's wife has returned a year after leaving him—but between her amnesia and the baby boy she's cradling, he's suddenly unsure of what really happened. Will he untangle the deception and lies surrounding her disappearance in time to salvage their marriage?

#2567 CONTRACT BRIDE

In Name Only • by Kat Cantrell

CEO Warren Garinger knows better than to act on his fantasies about his gorgeous employee Tilda Barrett, but when she needs a green card marriage, he volunteers to say, "I do." Once he's her husband, though, keeping his distance is no longer an option!

#2568 PREGNANT BY THE CEO

The Jameson Heirs • by HelenKay Dimon

Derrick Jameson dedicated his life to the family business, and all he needs to close the deal is the perfect fiancée. When the sister of his nemesis shows up, desperate to make amends, it's perfect...until a surprise pregnancy brings everyone's secrets to light!

SPECIAL EXCERPT FROM

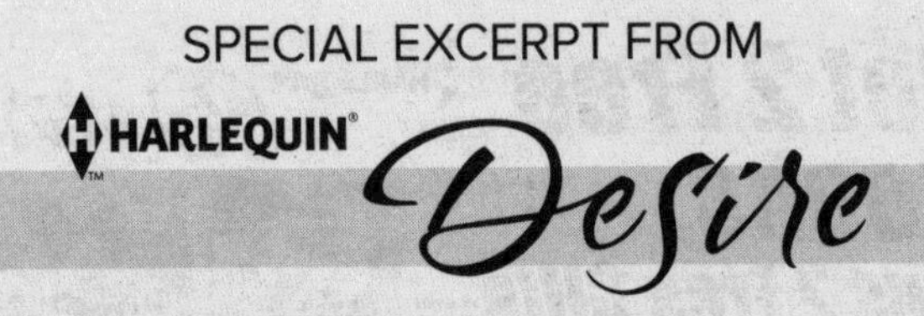

When Selena Jacobs's ex-husband shows up at his own funeral, it's her estranged best friend who insists on staying with her to keep her safe. But living with The One Who Got Away gets complicated when one night leads to an unexpected surprise...

Read on for a sneak peek at
THE RANCHER'S BABY
by New York Times *bestselling author Maisey Yates,*
the first book in the
***TEXAS CATTLEMAN'S CLUB: THE IMPOSTOR** series!*

She wandered out of the kitchen and into the living room just as the door to the guest bedroom opened and Knox walked out, pulling his T-shirt over his head—but not quickly enough. She caught a flash of muscled, tanned skin and...

She was completely immobilized by the sight of her best friend's muscles.

It wasn't like she had never seen Knox shirtless before. But it had been a long time. And the last time, he had most definitely been married.

Not that she had forgotten he was hot when he was married to Cassandra. It was just that...he had been a married man. And that meant something to Selena. Because it meant something to him.

It had been a barrier, an insurmountable one, even bigger than that whole long-term friendship thing. And now it wasn't there. It just wasn't. He was walking out of the guest bedroom looking sleep rumpled and entirely too lickable. And there was

HDEXP1217

just…nothing stopping them from doing what men and women did.

She'd had a million excuses for not doing that. For a long time. She didn't want to risk entanglements, didn't want to compromise her focus. Didn't want to risk pregnancy. Didn't have time for a relationship.

But she was in a place where those things were less of a concern. This house was symbolic of that change in her life. She was making a home. And making a home made her want to fill it. With art, with warmth, with knickknacks that spoke to her.

With people.

She wondered, then. What it would be like to actually live with a man? To have one in her life? In her home? In her bed?

And just like that she was fantasizing about Knox in her bed…